THE YOUNG UNDERGROUND

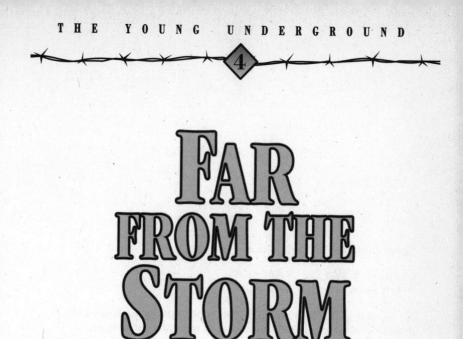

FAR FROM THE STORM

Robert Elmer

BETHANY HOUSE PUBLISHERS
MINNEAPOLIS, MINNESOTA 55438

Cover illustration by Chris Ellison

Published by Bethany House Publishers
A Ministry of Bethany Fellowship, Inc.
11300 Hampshire Avenue South
Minneapolis, Minnesota 55438

Printed in the United States of America.

Library of Congress Cataloging-in-Publication Data

Elmer Robert.
    Far from the storm / Robert Elmer.
       p.   cm. — (The young underground ; bk. 4)
    Summary: After World War II, Peter and Elise seek to discover who is trying to destroy Uncle Morten for his work with the Danish Underground.

    [1. Denmark—History—Fiction. 2. Brothers and sisters—Fiction. 3. Christian life—Fiction. 4. Mystery and detective stories.] I. Title. II. Series: Elmer, Robert. Young underground ; #4.
PZ7.E4794Far   1995
[Fic]—dc20   95–9623
ISBN 1-55661-377-6   CIP
                                      AC

To Kai—
My son, the encourager.

ROBERT ELMER has written and edited numerous articles for both newspapers and magazines in the Pacific Northwest. The YOUNG UNDERGROUND series was inspired by stories from Robert's Denmark-born parents, as well as friends who lived through the years of German occupation. He is currently a writer for an advertising agency located near Seattle. He and his wife, Ronda, have three children.

Contents

CITY OF CANDLES
MAY 4, 1945

No one in the city would be able to sleep that night, with all the shouting and singing.

"Is it true?" asked Peter's mom. "Is it really true?"

Mr. Andersen swept up Peter, his twelve-year-old twin sister, Elise, and their mother as they gripped one another's hands and danced around the living room. They skipped from room to room, father in the lead, trying not to trip over the cat. They laughed and sang every song they could remember until they were out of breath. It was Christmas and New Year's and everyone's birthday all at once.

"Hooo-rah!" someone whooped on the sidewalk below, and for a moment it sounded to Peter as if the man had jumped right up to their second-story living-room window.

Exhausted from dancing, Peter let go of his sister's and mother's hands and sank back into his father's brown corduroy easy chair to catch his breath. Everyone else in the family looked just

like him—smiling from ear to ear and red in the face from celebrating. Their cat, Tiger, found Peter's lap and made himself comfortable.

"Ow, Tiger," Peter yelped, pulling the striped kitten off his
chest. "Watch the claws." The two sat watching Mr. and Mrs. Andersen dance. Little Mrs. Andersen's red curls bobbed up and
down as she kept up with her tall husband. Their cheeks were
wet with tears, and they hugged each other for what must have
been the fiftieth time.

Elise ran to the window once more, almost doing a cartwheel
on her way there. Peter grinned. She would have to be careful her
long blond hair didn't catch fire from the three bright candles
shining in the windowsill.

Celebration candles glowed brightly in every window in the
city of Helsingor on that special night. Probably every window
in every city, every town, and every farm in Denmark had a can-
dle tonight, Peter thought. He pinched himself to make sure he
wasn't dreaming.

"Is it really true?" his mother asked once more.

"It's really true, Mom," answered Elise, staring out at the city
of candles.

Just like everyone else, they had heard the news on the British
radio that Friday night, May 4, 1945. The German troops who had
ruled their little country for five awful years had finally surrendered.

The war was over.

THE LONGEST NIGHT

Someone rapped on the front door. "I'll get it," Peter shouted as he launched himself from the easy chair toward the stairs.

"No, I will," said Elise. But Peter was already jumping down the stairs three at a time to the front door.

"Who could it be at this hour?" wondered their father from the living room. Peter couldn't remember when anyone had come to the door after nine at night. But the war was over—there were no more curfews to keep people off the streets after dark.

At the foot of the stairs, Peter noticed a folded piece of note-paper under the door. He stooped to pick it up and glanced at it for a name.

"Mr. Andersen," he read, squinting to make out the messy, childlike handwriting. Without reading the note, Peter stuffed it into his pocket and swung open the door.

"Hello?" Peter looked both ways down Axeltorv (Axel Tower) Street, but no one waited by the door. Across the street, a group of three or four men were laughing at one another as they made their way through the rainy night, but they paid no attention to Peter.

Without warning, a flash shot under his legs from behind, and Peter squeezed his legs together to keep Tiger from slipping outside.

"Tiger!" Peter quickly pulled the front door shut behind him—too late. "You're not supposed to go out at night!"

He ran down the sidewalk, calling after his cat, but Tiger had a mind of his own. In an instant, the cat was down the street and leaping over puddles as if it were a wonderful game.

Suddenly, a jeep full of German soldiers came screeching around the corner of Axeltorv Street, careening dangerously on two wheels. Peter could only motion helplessly as Tiger darted directly in front of the speeding vehicle. The driver didn't even slow down.

Peter closed his eyes, a cry choked somewhere in his throat. He wanted to plug his ears to keep from hearing the sickening thud as the jeep roared over his pet and continued down the wet street.

When Peter dared to look again, Tiger was lying in the middle of the street. He meowed in pain. Elise rushed up from behind and knelt in the water next to the crying animal.

"What happened?" Elise stroked Tiger gently. His side was scraped of fur and one leg was turned sideways at a crazy angle.

"Oh, Tiger, Tiger," Peter couldn't help crying. He put his head down close to the wounded cat's face. The rain pelted even harder.

"He's bleeding, Peter," said Elise. "We better get him inside."

Peter felt a wave of anger as he looked down the street. He wanted to throw something at the Germans in their jeep, but they had long since disappeared into the night.

"Your last night here," he yelled, "and you kill my cat!" He sobbed as he turned back to Tiger on the pavement, and his tears blended with the rain.

"He's not dead yet," comforted Elise.

Their front door opened, and their father ran out into the street.

"What's all the noise out here?" he asked. The twins didn't have to reply. "Try to keep the cat from moving," he directed.

"I think he broke his leg, or something," reported Elise. "And he's all scraped up."

Mr. Andersen nodded, dashed back into the house, and called to their mother for something. A moment later, the three of them carefully wrapped the cat in an old blanket, and Mr. Andersen gently carried the soaked animal back inside.

"You're going to be fine, little guy," Peter crooned as he walked with a hand on the blanket.

"How did he get out?" asked Mrs. Andersen as she wrapped a bandage around the mangled hip.

"I opened the door to see who had knocked," answered Peter, "and a jeep full of German soldiers came tearing around the corner. They didn't even slow down."

Their mother frowned as they turned the kitchen into an operating room. Elise cleared the dishes into the sink, Peter spread out the blanket, and their father carefully placed Tiger on the table.

"I think he looks worse than he is," Mr. Andersen finally announced after examining Tiger. "He's all scraped up, but it looks as though the worst damage is to his leg, or maybe his hip. We're going to have to set it."

"Do you know how?" questioned Elise.

"You forget I used to spend my summers at your great-grandfather's farm," he told them, pushing up his sleeves. "We can call the vet tomorrow, if he—"

Mrs. Andersen gave her husband a sharp look and shook her head, but Peter knew what his father was going to say. *If he makes it through the night.*

Tiger, his eyes wide, protested with a loud howl as they cleaned his wounds.

"Hold him, Elise!" ordered their dad when he was ready to set the hind leg. "And, Peter, get me a ruler, something straight. Two rulers, if you have them!"

Peter lost no time fetching a ruler out of his schoolbag, then grabbed two new pencils. The sound of the yowling cat was almost more than he could take, even from the other end of the apartment.

"Perfect," said their father, taking the pencils and the ruler. He placed them next to the leg of the cat and wrapped them firmly with white first-aid tape. Then he turned to Peter with a serious expression. "Let's put him in his basket and cover him up, son."

"He's going to be okay, isn't he?" asked Peter.

Mr. Andersen sighed and slumped his shoulders. "I wish I could promise you that. He has a good chance, but he got knocked around pretty badly."

Peter blew his nose and nodded.

"I'm sorry, Peter," his father continued. "Let's make him as comfortable as we can."

Peter obeyed, trying to fluff up the blanket in Tiger's cozy basket in the corner of the kitchen. He tucked in the blanket and tried to scratch the cat behind the ear. Normally Tiger would purr and give Peter a contented look. But this time the little animal's eyes were glassy and empty.

"Dad," Peter whispered over his shoulder, tears in his eyes, "he looks like he's dying."

Mr. Andersen looked up from the sink, where he was washing his hands. He dried them quickly, stepped over, and put an arm around Peter's shoulder. "He's probably in shock. We've done the best we can for him. If he makes it through the night, there's a good chance he'll be fine."

If he makes it through the night. Peter repeated his father's words in his mind as he lay in his bed. Everyone else had been asleep for hours. Even the singing outside their window had quieted down, replaced by a steady patter of spring rain.

But every time Peter closed his eyes, he saw the jeep speeding around the corner. More than once, he felt his ears turn hot with anger at the men who had mowed down Tiger without even a backward glance. *Why tonight?* he asked himself, replaying the image of Tiger's accident over and over in his mind.

"You're going to be fine, Tiger," he whispered to the darkness, and his whisper became a prayer.

"He *is* going to be fine, right, Lord? I didn't mean to let him out, but I guess it was my fault for not being more careful. And those Germans—if I was a little bigger, I would just strangle them—"

Peter caught his breath. The anger kept clawing at him. He reached out to the spot at the foot of his bed where Tiger usually slept. It felt cold.

"I'm sorry, God, for blowing it. But please don't let Tiger die. Look, I promise . . ." But Peter couldn't think of anything God might be interested in bargaining for.

Finally Peter threw back his covers and padded quietly down the hall to the kitchen. In the dark he listened for Tiger's familiar wheezing, but heard nothing. He got closer, on his knees, to make sure the cat was still in his basket. Tiger didn't—couldn't—move.

"Tiger?" Peter whispered. "Tiger?" He buried his face in the cat's fur and cried, sure his kitten was dead. But a faint rumbling from somewhere deep inside Tiger's chest made Peter catch his breath. He listened closer, not daring to hope. Then he was sure.

"Still purring, huh, little guy?" Peter whispered. He curled himself into a ball on the cool linoleum next to Tiger's basket and promptly fell asleep.

2

THE HOMECOMING

"Peter, wake up!"

Peter put his arm over his head and tried to pretend he couldn't hear his sister. His pillow was gone, and the bed seemed harder than usual.

"Peter," came the voice again. "What are you doing down there?"

He remembered where he was as he felt the cat move to lick at his bandages. A sandpaper tongue caught Peter on the ear, and he giggled.

"Hey, look," said Peter, unfolding stiffly from his spot on the floor. "He's awake."

His back ached, and the rug had left an imprint on his face. But when Peter opened his eyes to the early-morning sunshine and saw Tiger looking at him, it didn't seem to matter.

"Yeah, he sure is," said Elise, smiling. "But don't tell me you slept here on the floor in your pajamas." She crouched down to get a closer look, and Peter noticed she was already dressed in her Saturday pants and red blouse.

"Who, me?" he asked, stroking Tiger's head. The dazed look

that had frightened Peter the night before had been replaced with the kitten's usual curious expression. Tiger even tried to stand up once, but Peter gently held him down.

"Well, look who's awake," exclaimed Mrs. Andersen, coming into the kitchen.

"Mom, look!" Peter reported from the side of the cat basket. "He's okay!"

"Hmm," she replied, pouring some creamy milk into a bowl. "Let's see if his appetite is back."

Peter almost had to laugh as the kitten hungrily lapped up his milk. "He's even purring the way he used to."

But there was another sound that morning, too. From out in the street they could hear singing—loud singing, the same kind Peter had heard the night before.

"The sun is rising in the east . . ." sang the chorus underneath their window. Peter looked out to see a pack of men making their way on bicycles toward the harbor. Behind him, the phone rang.

"Really?" said Elise, shielding the heavy black receiver. She gave Peter a worried look, then turned her back to him and lowered her voice. "But, Britta, how do you know? Sure I knew your brother was in the army. But he just called you from Sweden? Just like that? Neat! Okay, we'll look for you—at least I think so. I'll have to ask my parents. Bye!"

"Ask your parents what?" asked Mr. Andersen. He buttoned the top button on his painting shirt as he walked into the kitchen.

Elise hung up the phone and glanced at her parents. "That was Britta from school," she told them uncertainly. "She says all the soldiers are coming back, and everybody in the whole city is going down to the harbor to meet them! Should we?"

Peter stood up and shook his head, feeling as if he were still in a fog. "Soldiers? What are you talking about? Aren't they all going back to Germany where they came from?"

"No, Peter." Elise slipped into her chair at the kitchen table. "*Danish* soldiers. Our soldiers. The ones who escaped to Sweden are coming home! And we're going down to the harbor to welcome them, right, Dad?"

Peter's parents looked at each other, and Mr. Andersen nodded as he mussed Peter's hair.

"What do you think, Peter?" he asked as he got down on his knees to examine Tiger. "Looks as though your kitten used up one of his nine lives, but he's pretty perky today."

"Yeah, Dad, he already drank a whole bowl of milk, and he even tried to stand up. Do you think that means he'll be okay?"

"Well, he sure looks better than he did last night. But he's not on his feet just yet. It'll take time for him to recover completely from that kind of accident."

"It wasn't an accident!" Peter blurted out. He started shaking as the picture of the racing German jeep replayed in his mind. "Those soldiers did it on purpose! They probably aimed straight for him."

"Okay, okay." Mr. Andersen straightened up and put his hand on Peter's shoulder. "Maybe you're right. But there's nothing we can do about it now. The war's over."

"Do you want to stay home, Peter?" asked Mrs. Andersen. "You don't have to go."

"No, I'm okay." Peter sniffled. "I'll get our Danish flags out of the closet." They had been saving the parade-sized flags for this occasion.

"Does that mean we're going?" asked Elise excitedly.

Mrs. Andersen held up a hand. "There's plenty of time for that. But first we need to eat, so all of you sit down while I fix something. And Peter, you better wash up."

Peter knew she was serious as she tried to rope her family back to the breakfast table—back to an orderly meal of boiled eggs on toast, juice, and fruit. But as he walked past the table, his hand brushed against a glass of milk his mother had just poured. And when he grabbed for it, the milk sprayed all over the table and onto the floor.

"Oh, Peter!" moaned Elise.

"Honestly, Peter," scolded their mother.

"Sorry," he apologized, pulling a dish towel from a hanger by the sink. Without thinking, he looked under the table for Tiger—the only one who enjoyed milk spills. "Tiger," he called.

Over in his basket, Tiger was looking longingly at the spill, as hungry as ever.

"Peter, he still can't walk," scolded Elise. "Let's not torture him."

Peter's father laughed, and they all joined in. "I think your Tiger is going to be okay," he finally told them, wiping his eyes with a napkin. "He knows he needs to help you clean up your spills."

With Tiger watching them from his basket, the mood at breakfast was filled with excitement. The phone rang twice more for Elise, and Mrs. Andersen chatted cheerfully about the warm weather.

"We better get going," Mr. Andersen finally announced, his mouth still full of toast. "There are going to be thousands and thousands of people down there."

"Arne," scolded Mrs. Andersen. "You're as bad as the kids. Let's at least finish what we're chewing before we all run out."

Mr. Andersen nodded sheepishly as he finished his juice.

"They're already out on the street." Elise pointed to the window.

After checking Tiger one last time and picking up the breakfast dishes, Peter and Elise raced down the stairs to the street. But Peter stopped short by their front door and slapped his forehead with the palm of his hand.

"The note!" he said, turning around to face the others as his parents caught up. "There was a note under the door last night. Just before Tiger got run over."

"What kind of a note?" asked Elise. "What did it say?"

Peter rummaged through his pockets, looking for the scrap of paper he had picked up during the excitement of the evening before. He pulled out a rock he had found down by the beach at the

Kronborg Castle, half of a comb, three rubber bands, the wheel from one of his toy cars, and a pencil stub. But no note.

"I thought I put it in here," he mumbled.

"With all the junk you carry around in your pockets, I don't see how you find anything in there," said Elise. "You probably lost it."

"I didn't lose it," insisted Peter, checking the other pocket. "It's got to be here." After retrieving a wad of string, two bottle caps, and five marbles, he pulled out a piece of crumpled, lined note-book paper.

"There, see?" He handed the paper to his father. "I didn't lose anything, Elise."

Outside, bright morning sunshine made up for the rain that had fallen all night. The old city's red-slate rooftops started to steam as the sun warmed them. But the Andersens hardly noticed with all the excitement.

They hurried down the crowded sidewalk, filled with people in a holiday mood. In the bakery two doors down from their apartment, Mr. Illeman had hand-lettered a large piece of paper with news of the German surrender. Around the edge of the sheet, he had arranged a dozen bright red and white paper Danish flags, exactly like those Peter and Elise carried. Elise nudged her brother as they walked.

"Is there anyone who hasn't heard, do you think?"

Peter looked at the crowds around them and shook his head. "Everybody in the whole world knows about this." He glanced over at their father, who was studying the note with a worried expression.

"What does it say, Dad?" asked Peter.

Their father didn't answer, only handed the note to Mrs. Andersen to read.

"What do you think, Karen?" their father asked. "Some kind of prank?"

"I don't know who would say something like that," answered Mrs. Andersen. "I don't think it's very funny."

"Can I see?" asked Peter, stepping up beside his mother.

She looked over at him with a frown. "Tell your friends we don't appreciate them leaving this kind of note on our doorstep," she told him. "They may think it's a joke, but . . ." Her voice trailed off, and she handed Elise the crumpled paper.

From his sister's worried expression, Peter knew it was no joke. He leaned in for a look, but he couldn't read the messy, childish handwriting.

"When Morten returns," Elise read, looking up with a frown.

"What else does it say?" Peter tried to make out the letters.

Elise wrinkled her nose and finished the note. "When Morten returns, he burns."

Elise handed him the note. "That's terrible, Peter. Did someone from your class write that?"

Peter looked closer, then shook his head. "I don't think so. Not unless it was Keld Poulsen. Nobody else I know would do something like this. Besides, who would know about Uncle Morten being gone?"

"Everyone knows that," replied Elise. "At least, anyone who knows him. And if they know that, they probably figure he's coming back soon."

Mr. Andersen still looked worried. "Well, Peter—or Elise—you tell whoever it is not to leave that kind of note on our doorstep again. I don't appreciate it one bit."

Peter took the note back and stuffed it into his pocket, still trying to think of who might have written such a horrible note.

By that time they had almost reached the harbor, and the crowd was elbow-to-elbow. So many happy people would not let them worry about a strange note for too long.

"This is the most people I've seen in one place since the neighborhood all-sing last March," yelled Peter's mother, looking more cheerful.

Everywhere around them, people were humming with excitement. Groups of people would suddenly burst into Danish songs they hadn't been allowed to sing during the war, patriotic songs like "We Love Our Land" or "King Christian Stood by the Tall Mast." With Tiger feeling better, Peter felt like singing again, too. But still, he was glad the Germans who had run over his cat were gone.

Everywhere in the crowd, everyone was asking the same question: "What time are the soldiers coming?"

Some people had heard nine o'clock, but nine had already come and gone. So had nine-thirty. A few small tugboats had ventured out of the harbor to see if any ships were coming.

"What we need to do is get to someplace high up so we can see everything," Elise told her brother. But their mother overheard and reached out to grab Peter by the back of the neck.

"You two stay right here," she told them. "I'm not going to lose you in this crowd."

But even though they stood on their tiptoes, Peter and Elise couldn't see what was going on. They were hemmed in by happy, singing people, nearly all of them waving flags like theirs. Flags that had been stored away for years, saved just for this day. Some of the flags were handmade out of red and white paper, the flag's white cross neatly cut out and pasted on top.

Behind them, people were hanging from nearly every window in the row of old red-brick five-story buildings that lined the harbor. Everywhere, everyone seemed to have a flag in hand. Teenage boys had crawled up on the steep roofs of a few buildings for a better view of the incoming ships. And in a couple of windows, people had draped large flags.

Then, almost as if on cue, everyone in the windows went crazy. They waved their flags wildly back and forth, waved their hands, and shouted more loudly than before.

At the entrance to the harbor where the harbor light stood guard, the same thing was happening at the end of the pier. The excitement spread through the crowd.

"They're coming!" announced Mr. Andersen, but everyone seemed to sense it at the same time. There was a tooting of foghorns from out in the harbor, and a sea of thousands of pretty Danish flags started waving.

All Peter and Elise could do was raise their flags and wait until something came close enough for them to see it. The heads of the man and woman ahead of him blocked Peter's view. When Mr. Andersen turned to say something, all Peter could hear was the deafening cheer of the crowd around them and the foghorns.

"Can you see anything?" Peter shouted at his father. Mr. Andersen couldn't hear, so Peter tugged at his shirt and repeated his question more loudly.

His father leaned down and spoke right into Peter's ear. "First ship is coming into the harbor. Big ferry full of Danish boys. The *Dan*."

Finally the ferry came in close enough to the large piers that everyone could see. The cheers seemed to become even more deafening as the black-and-white ferry with two tall smokestacks nudged a big pier.

Danish flags and uniformed young Danish soldiers draped the side of the ship. Everyone on the boat was smiling and waving in the biggest floating parade the city had ever seen. Peter and Elise jumped up and down in an effort to get a look at what was going on.

"Here, Elise," shouted their father, and he motioned for Peter's sister to climb onto his back as he crouched down. Even though she was taller than Peter, Elise gladly hopped up for her piggyback view.

Soon hundreds of smiling Danish troops were streaming out of the ferry, which was soon followed by many more ships. And still the crowd cheered and waved their flags. No one could get enough of the scene. And even though the police tried to keep a distance between the cheering crowds and the young soldiers, once in a while someone would break through and run up to the soldiers with flowers or even a kiss.

"My turn!" Peter tugged at his father's shirt and tried to get a piggyback view of his own. His father let Elise down and groaned.

"You kids are too heavy for this," he said. The crowd noise had died down for the moment. "Just for a minute, Peter."

From up on his father's back, Peter could finally see over the sea of people. Out in the harbor, a flotilla of ships, ferries, and assorted tugboats paraded toward land.

"I see the *Titan*," Peter pointed out a tugboat to his sister, and she nodded. "I think Grandfather's friend is steering."

"You don't see your grandfather, do you?" asked Peter's father.

Peter had already scanned the crowd in front of them. Grandfather's boathouse was around behind some of the buildings on the waterfront.

"Nope," answered Peter. "Just wall-to-wall people. I can almost see all the way out to the light. And at the rate the ships are coming in, pretty soon there's not going to be enough room in the harbor for all of them. But, whoa! Wait a minute—"

Peter nearly climbed over his father's shoulders as he tried to get a better look.

"Hey, you're getting too heavy," complained his dad. "I'm going to have to let you down."

"Wait a minute, Dad!" said Peter. "Do you see it?"

"No, but you've got to let go of my ears, Peter. Ouch!"

But Peter barely heard him. Holding on with one hand around his father's shoulder, he waved his flag as hard as he could and shouted at the top of his lungs.

"UNCLE MORTEN!"

Of course it was no use yelling. Peter strained his eyes to make out the little fishing boat that had just rounded the point. But he had seen it enough times to know the shape. It was blue and white—not gray like all the other boats. A woman was standing on the deck in front of the little steering house, waving her flag like everyone else.

"It's them!" Peter shouted excitedly as he slid down his

father's back. "Don't you see them?"

"I do," laughed his father. Mr. Andersen turned to his wife.

"My crazy brother is bringing the boat home in the middle of all this mess," he told her. "And it looks as if he's got his girlfriend with him, as well."

Elise grabbed Peter by the shoulders, holding him back for a minute.

"Are you sure it's them?" she asked. "Did you see Henrik?"

Peter shook his head, trying not to show his disappointment that his best friend was still in Sweden. "Uh-uh," he replied. "Just Uncle Morten and Lisbeth. Unless the Melchiors are sitting down. Maybe we just can't see them."

"Maybe," Elise replied with a touch of hope in her voice. "You never know."

The four Andersens tried to push through the crowd with Peter in the lead, his father trying to keep a hand on Peter's shoulder.

"Wait for us, Peter," he called after his son.

But there was no slowing Peter. There was still a chance that Henrik might be with Peter's uncle.

"Excuse me. Pardon me," said Peter, trying to part the crowd. But the closer they got to the pier, the more tightly packed the people were. There was no way to get through.

"Peter, look over here," called Elise from somewhere behind them.

Peter and his dad turned to see that Elise had found a break in the crowd leading off to the side. They turned, squeezed past a group of people with bicycles, and came around through a boat-yard.

"They're going to try to dock where they always used to," guessed Peter, "but it's already full of boats."

"I don't think that's going to stop anyone," answered their father, holding tightly to their mother's hand as they pushed through the crowd of people. "Looks as if everyone is rafting up and double-parking here. We'll just have to step over a few boats that are tied up to one another side by side."

"But where are they now?" asked Mrs. Andersen, scanning the harbor. "I lost track of them."

"I see them!" announced Elise, standing on top of a large wheelbarrow-shaped maintenance cart. "They have a flag flying from the mast."

"Where?" asked Peter. "Really?"

He jumped up on the cart with her, but it wasn't big enough to hold them both. Peter waved his arms like windmills as the twins came crashing down on top of their father.

"Hold on there!" laughed Mr. Andersen, pulling them to their feet.

Peter still had his eyes on the harbor. "Sorry, Dad. But I saw them, too."

"All right, I believe you," he replied. "Just follow me now."

The four Andersens scrambled down the pier, which was low in the water, and they hopscotched across the back decks of three tugboats that were tied up side by side. In the scramble of boats and people, no one seemed to mind. Everyone was still waving and cheering.

Except Keld Poulsen. Peter caught just a glimpse of him as he checked over his shoulder to see if Elise was keeping up. The school bully, the one person who had caused the twins so much trouble, was staring glumly in their direction from the middle of a crowd of people. It didn't surprise Peter that Keld was empty-handed, the only person around who wasn't holding or waving a flag. The boy looked strangely out of place, like someone lost in a foreign country. Instantly, Peter looked away. But when he peeked back, Keld was gone.

"Who are you looking at, Peter?" asked Elise from right behind him.

"I just saw the Nazi," answered Peter. "What's he doing down here, do you think?"

"You mean Keld Poulsen?" Elise glanced at him, and Peter nodded and frowned.

But in the noise and excitement, he could only think about one thing at a time. And when he saw his uncle's battered blue and white fishing boat, he jumped into the air like a cheerleader, waving his hands wildly.

"We're here!" yelled Peter.

"Uncle Morten!" added Elise.

At the wheel of the *Anna Marie*, Uncle Morten knew just where he was going. The tall, broad-shouldered man leaned out the window of the deckhouse and steered straight for the larger tugboat where the Andersens stood.

Beside him stood Lisbeth von Schreider, the woman who had escaped to Sweden with Uncle Morten several months before. Her dark, shoulder-length hair flew in the wind, and her pretty smile seemed to match the mood of the celebration.

Peter scanned the deck hopefully one more time. Maybe Henrik was sitting down somewhere. But unless Henrik and his parents were down in the fishhold—the way they had traveled to Sweden—they were not on board the *Anna Marie*. Peter felt as if someone had just doused his excitement with ice water.

"They're not here," he told his sister, shaking his head. "I thought maybe they would be."

Elise quickly scanned the boat. "Maybe they're—"

"They're not," Peter repeated. "They're not on the boat."

At the last moment, Uncle Morten veered sharply to the left, lining the right side of his boat up with the side of the tug. In a froth of foam, he yanked the boat into reverse, and the *Anna Marie* slid sideways into place, barely missing the side of the other boat.

"Here, grab a line," he called. "Lis, toss them the bow line."

Lisbeth scrambled to the front of the boat to toss a coil of rope to Elise, who was standing at the railing of the tugboat where they would tie up.

"Welcome home," yelled Mr. Andersen as he vaulted over to the smaller boat. Peter wasn't sure he had ever seen his father so happy, and in a moment his father and uncle were slapping each other on the back and laughing.

They looked so much alike, and yet so different. The banker and the fisherman. Peter's clean-cut father and the uncle who had worked with the Underground resistance against the Germans. But it was obvious they were brothers.

Peter fumbled to find a place to tie the rope from the back end of the boat. *Where's Henrik?* he wondered. *Maybe Uncle Morten left too soon, and Henrik couldn't get a ride back. Maybe he's getting ready to leave Sweden even now with his parents.* It seemed like a very long time since his Jewish friend had had to flee to Sweden. Actually it had been about a year and a half.

His sister bent down next to where Peter was tying and untying a knot. "Go ahead, Peter," she urged him. "I'll take care of this."

Peter shook his head and mumbled that he could take care of it okay. Then he tied the knot for the third time, untying it once more.

"Peter!" called Uncle Morten. "How's my favorite nephew?"

Peter looked up shyly as Uncle Morten climbed up and over the railing of the tugboat to give Peter a giant bear hug.

"Fine," replied Peter. "I'm doing okay."

Uncle Morten held Peter at arm's length and tried to look him in the face. "Your dad told me about Tiger."

Peter nodded and looked down.

"Remember how he saved my life in the German prison?" Uncle Morten looked around at the others. "Did Peter ever tell you how his little alley cat saved my life? Yes?"

"Part hound dog," joked Mr. Andersen, his arm around Uncle Morten's shoulder. "So how in the world did you get back to Denmark so quickly, little brother? We had no idea you were coming back so soon until Peter saw you chasing all these big boats into the harbor."

"We weren't going to waste a minute more over there," answered Uncle Morten. "The Swedes were great to us, but it's been a long two months for Lisbeth and me. As soon as we heard our boys were getting ready to come home, we waited right in the harbor with them."

Couldn't he have waited just a little longer for Henrik? thought Peter.

"Then when the announcement came yesterday," continued Uncle Morten, "we hopped into the boat. I just wish Henrik and his parents could have been with us."

He looked at Peter once again with a serious expression.

"You probably don't know that Henrik's father is very sick, Peter. They have to stay in Sweden for a while longer."

"Sick?" Peter gulped.

"I think it's his heart. The Swedish doctors are doing everything they can to help him. I talked with Henrik's mom on the phone, and they're doing okay." He looked around. "But where's Dad?"

"We haven't seen Grandfather yet," answered Elise from the deck of the tug, where she was tying down the fourth rope to secure their fishing boat. "But he has to be around here somewhere."

"Probably shooing people away from the boathouse," joked Mr. Andersen, looking over the happy scene. "Hard to believe it's all over now."

Lisbeth still hadn't said anything. She just stood on the boat, gripping the handrail and staring with wide, misty eyes at the sea of flags and people all over the waterfront.

Every few minutes, another shout went up as people welcomed the soldiers getting off ferries and transports. Everywhere there was singing. But Lisbeth didn't say anything; she just let the tears run down her cheeks.

"Here, Lisbeth," said Peter's mother, coming up to her. "This is a crazy welcome home, isn't it? You probably just want to get back to your apartment. Peter, why don't you help your uncle and Lisbeth with their bags?"

Lisbeth buried her face in a handkerchief. "I'm sorry. I just wasn't sure what it would be like when we got home. Or if we would ever get home at all. And now all this."

"It's okay, Lisbeth." The way Uncle Morten said it surprised Peter—he sounded kind of like Peter's dad did when talking to his mom. Uncle Morten stepped up to Lisbeth and put his arm around her shoulder. "We're home."

No Accident

Boats were still coming in when Peter and Elise escaped to the boathouse that night to check on the pigeons. Already, Lisbeth had left for Copenhagen to see her parents, while Uncle Morten had gone to visit friends after an early dinner with the Andersens.

The King of Denmark had been on the radio earlier that day, telling the whole country that their prayers for freedom had finally been answered. But Peter didn't feel much like celebrating.

He stared moodily into the cage at the three birds—Peter, Elise, and Henrik each had one. "First Tiger gets run over, then Henrik isn't coming back. Any more bad news?"

"Well, at least the pigeons are okay," suggested Elise as she looked over the birds. "There's Number One, Number Two, and Number Three. They still have all their feathers. In fact, I think your Number Two is getting a little fat from not flying."

Peter nodded absently and held out a dried pea, trying to get his bird to eat it through the chicken-wire divider that stretched from the floor to the ceiling. It sounded as if people were still walking around outside the boathouse, but when Peter checked, no one was there.

"I heard the British are already in Copenhagen," added Elise, "and they're supposed to be here by tomorrow."

Peter tossed the pea toward the pigeon, which fluttered its wings before chasing the food. "Really? Where'd you hear that?"

"Out on the street. Some people passing by were talking."

Peter managed a weak smile. "Everybody's talking, or yelling, or singing. I've never heard so much noise."

"Or seen so many flags," added Elise. She glanced out the window at the darkening street. "But it looks like people are going back to town. I don't see anyone out there right now."

"We should be getting home, too," said Peter. "There's no sense in just sitting here in this dark boathouse."

"Maybe we should check the *Anna Marie* before we run home," suggested Elise.

"Sure." Peter jumped up from his chair and started for the door. He sniffed the air for a moment.

"Do you smell that?" he asked his sister, sniffing again. "I think something's burning."

Elise wrinkled her nose and squinted. "I smell it too," she said, following Peter out the door. "But it's not coming from here."

They both saw the smoke at the same time, and they leaped down the gangway to the dock.

"Where's it coming from?" yelled Peter.

Elise didn't answer. By that time they could both see a yellow-orange glow behind the three tugs that were piled up next to their dock. Peter hurdled over a coiled pile of thick towing rope on the deck of the first tug, then over the railing of the second boat. By the time they reached the third and largest boat, there was no doubt where the flames were coming from.

For a moment Peter didn't know what to do. A small fire was licking through the inside of the *Anna Marie*. Then the front windshield shattered, sending flames and more smoke outside.

"I'll go get help," yelled Elise. But before she turned around she grabbed Peter by the shoulder. "I'll be *right* back. Don't do anything stupid!"

Peter nodded and looked around to see if anyone else had seen the fire. He and Elise were sheltered behind the three tugboats, but it wouldn't be long before someone out in the half-dark harbor noticed what was going on.

"A bucket," he told himself, running in circles around the deck of the third tugboat. "I've got to find a bucket!"

But he couldn't find any buckets on the deck of the third boat, so he jumped to the next one. Next to the large deckhouse he spied a mop handle sticking out of a bucket.

"There!" He grabbed the metal pail, dumped the mop, and vaulted back over to the boat that was tied to the *Anna Marie*. If the fire got any bigger, they would probably have to untie the boats from one another. The flames from inside the deckhouse licked at the window on the right side, blackening the glass.

"I can't believe it," fumed Peter as he lowered the bucket into the inky black harbor water between the boats. He wished he could reach it on his knees, but the sides of the boats were too high. He yanked up the bucket as fast as he could, but it caught on the tug's railing just before he got his hand on it and dumped most of the water.

"Stupid!" Peter scolded himself. Tears stung his eyes as the smoke from the fire blew toward him. Finally Peter managed to pull up a bucket of water and heave it with all his might at the flames. Most of it fell short.

There has to be a better way, he thought as he lowered the bucket for another try. On the next throw he managed a little better, causing some of the flames to falter and hiss. But the fire was growing larger every second. He glanced around to see if Elise had returned.

"I need help," he mumbled, heaving another bucketful with all his strength. But it seemed to do no good. He threw each bucketful more desperately as he watched the flames lick higher and higher.

"Elise, where are you?" he called into the fire. With the next throw he lost his grip on the bucket—sending it sailing straight into the flames. But he yanked it back with the rope before it disappeared.

"Peter!" came a voice from behind him. "Are you still here?"

Peter glanced over his shoulder just in time to see Elise try to hurdle the railing of the third tugboat. But her foot caught on the railing, and she did a twist in the air and landed on her back a few feet behind Peter.

Peter rushed over to where Elise lay on the deck, arching her back in pain.

"Elise! You okay?" He wasn't sure what she had broken. She tried to answer, but only gasped.

"Say something!"

"I'm okay," she finally croaked. "Wind."

"Wind?"

"It knocked the wind out of me . . . I'm okay. I got help."

They looked up at the dock to see several men running toward the burning boat. "The hose—over here!" one of them shouted.

Another jumped over to the boat where they were, dragging a fire hose from the other side of the boatyard.

Peter looked up at the dock, then over toward the burning boat, and hopped up. Elise tried to stand, and he pulled her up.

"I'm okay, really," she insisted, but Peter could tell she was in a lot of pain. Still, there was no time to discuss it. The twins helped as much as they could, pulling the heavy canvas hoses from boat to boat. Moments later crew members were swarming over their tugboats while the boats' captains shouted orders. An engine roared to life, brilliant deck floodlights winked on, and the tugboat closest to them tried to untangle itself from the *Anna Marie*.

"Right in the middle," urged one of the firemen to the man beside him. "Hit it right in the middle!"

"It won't reach," replied the other man. "The hose isn't long enough!"

They had pulled their hoses from the boatyard to the limit, but the best they could do was stand in the middle of the second boat and arch the water as far as they could. The water wouldn't quite reach. Peter heard more glass breaking.

"They're not going to make it," Peter yelled at his sister over the roar of the tugboat engines. "I'm going back to the bucket!"

As the boats were coming apart, Peter scrambled from deck to deck once more. He retrieved his bucket from the deck of the third boat while one crewman loosed the ropes that held his boat to the *Anna Marie*.

"Out of the way, kid," barked the crewman. Peter jumped to the rear deck of his uncle's fishing boat—just out of reach of the flames—and started to throw what water he could on the fire.

"Hey, get away from there," warned the same crewman, but Peter only dipped more water.

A moment later Elise joined him in the battle.

"Here, let me try it," she told him, mopping water off her face with his sleeve. "We're going to have to get closer."

The fire was hotter than Peter expected, and he pulled instinctively away as the flames met him head-on. Elise madly pitched water at the flames, but they only seemed to lick up the water. Someone yelled at them as she reached down into the water for yet another bucketful.

"Peter!" boomed the big voice of Uncle Morten. "Elise! You kids get back!"

Peter turned to see his Uncle Morten and Grandfather Andersen jumping down from the large tug next to the *Anna Marie*.

Elise looked back, but didn't stop. Uncle Morten pulled her back from the edge of the flames, looking her right in the face.

"Okay, let's make a chain," said Uncle Morten. He was already soaked from the rain of the fire hose, just like everyone else.

They formed two bucket lines. Peter scooped and handed his bucket to Grandfather on one side, while Elise scooped and handed to Uncle Morten on the other.

"We're holding it," yelled Grandfather, his voice hoarse.

A moment later Peter was hit in the back by a stream of water. He stumbled on the slippery deck and nearly went over. A man struggling with a hose nozzle appeared above them on the railing of the larger boat.

"Stand out of the way," he called to the bucket brigade. "We put both hoses together!"

Peter scrambled to his feet. In a minute, the flames inside the boat's steering house were reduced to a smoldering skeleton of wood.

"Are you okay, Peter?" asked Grandfather, coughing and wheezing.

Peter nodded, but held on to Grandfather's arm. Everyone was soaked to the skin, and Elise was coughing, too. They stood back from the steam.

"Look at your boat, Grandfather," moaned Peter. He rested his head on his grandfather's shoulder. "We were in the boathouse when it started."

"We could have stopped it," added Elise, sending a last bucketful of spray at the boat, "if we had just gone down to check a few minutes earlier." She threw the bucket to the deck.

"Yeah," agreed Peter. "Just a few minutes earlier."

Uncle Morten didn't seem to hear them as he stared at his steaming boat. He shook his head as he surveyed the wrecked deckhouse.

"Pretty bad, right?" asked Peter. He already knew the answer to his question.

Grandfather leaned over and tried to open what was left of the side door, but it fell off its hinges and splashed into the harbor. The inside was blackened to a crisp, and the flames had started a hole through the roof.

"There's a lot to clean up," he pronounced. "But we can fix it." Peter didn't think his grandfather sounded convinced.

"One thing's sure," said Uncle Morten. "If the kids hadn't been here, we wouldn't have a boat to fix up at all."

Grandfather took one of the buckets and doused a hot coal next to the boat's steering wheel. Like everyone else, his face was streaked with soot and his clothes were soaked. "We're going to have to find out how this started, Morten."

Peter and Elise looked at each other.

"The note!" Peter shouted, glancing back at the pier. People were starting to go home, and the men were rolling up their hoses.

"What note?" asked Uncle Morten.

Peter pushed Elise's shoulder. "You tell them."

"No, you. You're the one who found it."

Peter frowned. "We got this dumb note on the door last night, Uncle Morten. It said something like, 'When Morten comes back—' "

"It said, 'When Morten returns, he burns,' " finished Elise.

"Yeah, that's it," agreed Peter. "Dad didn't think it meant anything since it looked as though a kid wrote it, but we wondered how anyone would know you were coming back. We didn't even know ourselves."

Uncle Morten looked sideways at the twins and frowned. "Everyone is coming back. It's a safe guess that I would, too. I agree with your dad—it sounds like a kid's prank to me, too. I wouldn't worry about it."

"But, Uncle Morten," protested Elise. "Don't you think it could have something to do with the fire?"

"Why would anyone want to do this?" Uncle Morten swept his hand over the boat, then shook his head. "No. We'll keep our eyes open, but I don't think you kids need to worry about any of this."

But Peter and Elise weren't convinced.

"I still think the note has something to do with the fire," whispered Elise as they watched their uncle and grandfather secure the boat. The men with the tugboats shut down their engines and retied their mooring lines.

"Still, why would someone want to burn the *Anna Marie*?" asked Peter. "I don't get it. And if someone is trying to get at him, who would know Uncle Morten is already back?"

"I don't know," replied Elise, looking down at a light's reflection in the water. "But maybe . . ." She dropped to her knees. "Maybe there are some clues. Here, give me that bucket. I think I see something floating down there."

Peter gave his sister the bucket he had used to try to put out the fire. "What do you need it for?"

"Maybe it's a clue."

She carefully lowered the bucket into the harbor, dipping it several times in the water between the boats. Peter tried to make out what she was fishing for, but he could see nothing in the dark water.

"Aha," she finally said, pulling up the bucket. Elise brought it up on deck and gently poured out the water. She pulled out what looked like a man's shoe.

"A shoe?" asked Peter.

"It was just floating there. I think it might be a clue." Elise held it up to one of the lights and turned it over. "It hasn't been in the water too long. Maybe the person who set the fire lost it trying to get away." Then she looked over at her uncle.

"Hey, Uncle Morten," said Peter. "Elise just found a clue."

"Looks like a plain black street shoe to me," replied their uncle. He was right about that. The shoe was a black leather loafer, the kind worn by hundreds of men in the city. "And like I said, we don't even know how the fire started. You sure you didn't see anyone when you first got down to the boats?"

Peter tried to put together the pieces of what he had just seen, wishing he would have witnessed something. But no. He couldn't remember seeing anyone when they first saw the flames and smelled the smoke. He shook his head.

"I can't think of anything." Then he remembered and put up his finger. "But I did see Keld Poulsen down at the docks this afternoon."

Uncle Morten threw a piece of the burned boat down to the deck and gave Peter a funny look. "Keld and the rest of the city of Helsingor, Peter. Don't try too hard to be a detective. I'm just glad I was close by at your grandfather's apartment when it happened."

Don't try too hard to be a detective. Peter looked down as his ears heated up in embarrassment. He turned when he heard someone clattering over the boats toward them.

"Hello, over there!" called a middle-aged man in dirty blue coveralls. Peter recognized the unshaven man as the harbor security guard. "Looks like we had some trouble here."

Peter wondered how he could be so cheery after something so awful.

"Thanks, Madsen," answered Grandfather, looking up at the man and shielding his eyes from the spotlight. "But I'm afraid you're too late."

"Sorry I wasn't here a little earlier." Madsen's apologetic smile revealed tobacco-stained teeth. He leaned over the railing of the tugboat to inspect the damage. "Any idea what started the fire? Bad wiring?"

Uncle Morten crossed his arms over his chest and shook his head. "Nope. The wiring was fine."

"Well, it was a pretty old thing anyway, wasn't it?"

Peter saw Uncle Morten bristle. "The only reason it looks a little run down is because it's been in Sweden for the past year and a half. I really can't imagine a fire starting itself like that."

"Me neither," replied Madsen. "But I saw it happen once over on Bornholm Island a few years ago. Fire started itself, just like that, in a pile of rags someone had been using for painting. Spontaneous combustion, they called it."

"Hmm." Uncle Morten frowned.

"You had some rags in the boat?" pressed Madsen.

"A couple, maybe," admitted Uncle Morten. "But I don't think—"

"Well, whatever set this fire," added Grandfather Andersen, "we'll have the boat rebuilt in no time."

"I don't think it was paint rags," pronounced Elise. "I think someone set it."

"That so?" drawled Mr. Madsen, scratching his neck. "I expect I would have seen someone when I was on my rounds. I'm around here all the time." He pointed at the dark outline of a small metal-sided warehouse across the boatyard and some distance from Grandfather Andersen's dock and boathouse.

"Elise is right," insisted Peter. "The guy even dropped his shoe!"

"Oh?" Mr. Madsen perked up. "I'll need to see that."

Elise was bent over something on the deck, but she slowly straightened with the shoe in her hand. Without a word she held it out for Mr. Madsen to see, and he leaned over to snatch it out of her hand.

"Looks like an ordinary shoe to me," observed Mr. Madsen, turning it around.

"That's what we told the kids," answered Uncle Morten. "Not much of a clue, just trash floating in the harbor."

"Humph." The security officer held up the shoe and inspected it more carefully. "You're right. I pick up this kind of trash around the docks all the time. Comes from those sailor slobs on their ships. I'll throw it out for you."

"We can do that—" began Elise. "Can I have it, please, Mr. Madsen?"

Mr. Madsen had started back across the deck of the tugboat, but he looked back and shrugged, then tossed the shoe back to Elise. "Suit yourself, young lady."

Everyone watched in silence as he turned on his heel and picked his way back across the tugboat decks, grumbling something about litter and sloppy sailors.

"He's an odd one," whispered Peter after Mr. Madsen had disappeared.

"I don't like him," added Elise.

"Hush, you two," scolded Grandfather Andersen. "He does a good job. He's always taking care of things. Keeps the waterfront clean."

Elise frowned but didn't say anything else. Grandfather turned to Uncle Morten.

"We're not going to accomplish anything else here tonight," he declared. "This fire is out cold. Let's come back in the morning."

"Okay, just a minute," replied Uncle Morten. "I'm going to put this fender here between the boats. You should rest. You're still not feeling well."

"I'm fine," coughed Grandfather. "I'm an old Viking."

Peter looked around the ruined boat once more and shook his head sadly. Seeing the *Anna Marie* like that almost made him want to cry. Then someone in the tugboat switched off a light, leaving them alone under an inky blue-red sky and the streetlight on the pier. He shivered right down to his damp, squishy socks in the early evening chill.

"Let's go." Peter turned to Elise, and they climbed carefully over the boats to the dock.

"Come back tomorrow," Uncle Morten called after them. "You can help us start cleaning this up after church."

Church. For once, there would probably be a lot of people in the city's big beautiful cathedrals. Tomorrow they would celebrate their new freedom. Peter looked forward to seeing his uncle there. It would be the first time in months all their family went together.

But for now, it was still Saturday night in the harbor city, and everyone on the streets was in a celebrating mood. Two sooty wet kids walking quickly along the narrow sidewalks didn't fit into the scene.

"Let's hurry," said Elise, speeding up to a trot. She held the old shoe in one hand. "We need to get home so we can tell Mom and Dad what happened to the boat."

"I wish we could tell them who did it," answered Peter. It occurred to him that the person who had set the fire was still around somewhere. Maybe walking along the same street, or in one of the many groups of singing, celebrating people. Unless it was Keld Poulsen.

"Wait up!" Peter called, quickening his step.

They turned a corner, trotting past windows full of flags and candles. Peter's shoes made waterlogged squishing sounds as he tried to keep up with his sister.

"Think it was a teenager out making trouble?" he asked.

Elise shook her head as they slowed to a walk. "If it was someone just making trouble, he wouldn't have picked the *Anna Marie*. What I can't understand is why the person didn't wait until later, when no one would have been around. It doesn't make any sense."

"Yeah, I know," replied Peter with a shrug. "I just can't imagine who would want to do something like that. Who hates us that much, besides Keld Poulsen?"

"I don't know. But we're going to figure it out," Elise promised. "Maybe we'll find some more clues down by the boat tomorrow after church."

"Maybe," repeated Peter.

"All we have to do is find another shoe, then see if they match . . ."

"Like Cinderella?"

Elise had a far-off look that told him she was coming up with a plan. Peter knew her well enough not to ask what she was thinking. When Elise was ready, she would tell him.

4

FORGET AND FORGIVE

"I haven't heard so much singing in church since . . . since . . ."
Grandfather Andersen tugged at his chin, searching for the rest
of his sentence. Peter thought he looked different leading the Andersens out the double doors of the Helsingor cathedral in a gray
Sunday suit.

It wasn't the small church his uncle used to attend, but this
was a special occasion. Even Peter's parents came along. Peter
enjoyed the singing. He especially liked looking up into the peak
of the high arched ceiling.

Peter's banker father was more used to wearing a suit, but he
tugged at the starched collar of his shirt as he stepped out into
the Sunday noon sunshine. "I can't remember seeing so many
people in the church at one time, either. I'd think people would
have sung themselves hoarse by now."

Peter's dad looked over at Uncle Morten. "I just hope it wasn't
spoiled by—"

"Look, Arne," interrupted Uncle Morten. "I've waited a long
time to go to church again with you and the whole family. How
long has it been since I was captured, a year and a half?" He made

a sweeping motion with his hand at the city, which still seemed alive with singing.

"Finally we can walk around without ugly German swastika flags hanging all over the city. Nothing—no one—is going to spoil this day. Not the Germans. Not a fire. Nothing!"

"But what are you going to do without your boat, Uncle Morten?" Elise asked. She was wearing her best dress, a robin's egg blue with white lace trim and white shoes.

"This family worries too much!" Uncle Morten grinned. "Besides, we still have the boat. We just have a little fixing-up to do. I was getting tired of painting that old cabin over and over again, anyway. How many times have we changed colors, Dad—ten? This will give us a chance to fix it up again before Lisbeth returns, before the—"

Uncle Morten suddenly looked embarrassed, and he glanced down at his feet, stumbling for a word.

"Before the what?" asked Mr. Andersen, grinning. "Is my little brother finally going to make a public announce—ow!"

Mr. Andersen looked quickly over at the twins' mother, who had just planted her elbow in his side. She gave him a warning look, and he put up his hands in surrender.

"Okay," he told her apologetically. "Morten was going to say it anyway."

"What are you going to announce?" Peter asked Uncle Morten, but the deep, brassy clang of the cathedral's noon bell drowned out his question.

While Peter waited as the twelve bongs echoed through the narrow cobblestone streets, he realized the answer to his question.

"What was that, Peter?" asked Uncle Morten when the vibrations had died down.

"Uh, nothing," replied Peter. "Nothing at all."

Peter was sorry he had asked, especially since it was obvious what Uncle Morten had started to say. *I'll bet he and Lisbeth talked about getting married when they were stuck in Sweden these past few months*, he thought.

Peter and Elise liked Lisbeth von Schreider, the woman who had helped them escape the terrifying bombing of the German headquarters in Copenhagen only two months earlier. She had never been afraid to stick up for what was right. And Peter admired her for the way she had stood up to the Germans when she worked in the German headquarters as a spy for the Danish Underground.

Elise and Lisbeth had also quickly become friends, right from the time Lisbeth had invited them into her Bible study. They both liked the same kind of jazz music.

Peter supposed that if Uncle Morten had to be interested in someone, Lisbeth might be nice to have around. His uncle had always been single, after all. But Peter wrinkled his nose at the thought of calling her "Aunt" Lisbeth. It was a new idea.

"*Aunt* Lisbeth?" He was talking to himself.

"What's wrong with that?" asked Elise. "I think it would be fun to have an Aunt Lisbeth!"

"I guess," answered Peter. "I just never thought of it that way before. Most people already have their aunts and uncles before they're born. It's kind of weird. . . ." He wrinkled his nose again, then stopped as Uncle Morten let the other adults walk ahead. Their uncle waited for the kids to catch up.

"Did I hear my name mentioned? You two kids gossiping about your poor uncle behind his back?"

Peter couldn't help grinning. "Well, kind of."

"Aha!" replied Uncle Morten. "Secrets, probably all of them false. What did you say about me?"

"We were just wondering about you and . . ." Elise looked up shyly.

"About me and what?" asked Uncle Morten, a smile playing on his face. "Or should I ask, about me and whom?"

But his playful grin disappeared as two uniformed men stepped out of a shop directly in front of their group. The German soldiers looked dirty and tired, and one struggled with a bulging duffel bag. The other, a young boy, carried a worn cardboard box. They were obviously leaving for home, like all the other defeated German soldiers stationed in the city.

"Peter, watch out!" warned Elise. Without realizing it, Peter bowled straight into the younger soldier, sending the box flying from the man's arms. In a moment, the sidewalk was filled with socks, shirts, hats, underwear, several books—probably everything the young man owned.

Peter stood statue-still for a moment. He stared straight into the face of the young German, a boy not five years older than Peter. Seeing the uniform, all he could think of was the jeep of German soldiers who had run over Tiger.

His panic told him to run, but his feet felt glued to the pavement.

"Peter," said Uncle Morten quietly. "Let's help this boy with his—"

He just couldn't. Without a word, Peter jumped over a pile of shirts and ran down the street as fast as his legs would carry him.

Up ahead a half block, Grandfather and the others hadn't noticed what had happened. As he neared them, Peter slowed to a walk and caught his breath, then looked quickly over his shoulder.

Uncle Morten was on all fours, helping the Germans with their scattered luggage. Elise, too, was helping them gather some of the clothes.

Peter took a step in their direction, then held back. Like one magnet repelled by another, he couldn't make himself move any closer.

Peter said nothing when Elise and Uncle Morten caught up. He just kept his eyes glued to the sidewalk.

But inside their apartment, Elise stopped her brother at the door to his room. He tried to close his door, but she held it with her foot.

"Are you okay?" she asked him. "How come you ran?"

Peter didn't look at his sister. He tried halfheartedly to close his door, but not hard enough to push Elise away.

"I have to get my work clothes on."

"You left Uncle Morten and me all by ourselves."

"Did he say anything?"

"Not much. I think the soldiers were kind of scared."

"Of what? They're the ones with the guns. They're the ones that almost killed Tiger." He still felt hot around the ears, hot with anger.

Elise closed her eyes and nodded. "I guess Uncle Morten—"

"What?"

"Nothing. I shouldn't say."

"Come on, Elise," insisted Peter. "What did he say?"

"Okay. He said the war's over. And he said you looked as if you might have a hard time forgiving the Germans."

"That's not true," replied Peter, defensively. "I'm trying to forget all about it."

"Not forget, Peter. Forgive. They are two different things."

Two different things? Peter shut the door behind him and leaned against it with a sigh. The last thing he wanted to think about was forgiving the Germans, especially not the ones who had run over Tiger and left him in the street. He would rather just forget about it and watch it fade into the past.

Only trouble was the more he tried to forget about it, the worse it all seemed to become.

5

CLUE NUMBER TWO

On the way down to the boat after a midday meal, Peter was glad no one said anything about what happened on the way home from church. He stayed away from his parents and Elise all the way down to the dock.

When they reached the *Anna Marie*, everyone just stood and stared.

"Oh, Uncle Morten," groaned Elise. "It's awful!"

"Looks worse in the daytime," added Peter. "Kind of like a face without a nose."

Uncle Morten climbed down into the wreckage and kicked at the charred remains of the deckhouse. The hull of the boat looked okay, and the deck had held up. But the deckhouse—the part of the cabin built around the steering wheel—was completely ruined.

"Here, see?" Uncle Morten called up to the rest of them. He twirled what was left of the steering wheel. "It's not so bad. The wheel still turns. I'll bet the engine still runs just fine."

Grandfather Andersen climbed down, and the rest of them

followed. He tested the floorboards gently; they seemed to hold his weight.

"Well," he pronounced with a deep breath and a cough, "if we're going to get this thing fixed, we'll need everyone's help."

The rest of that afternoon was spent pulling off blackened boards and carting them up to the boatyard next to their shed. Elise and Peter also took turns on the pump, removing all the water that the firemen had poured in the evening before.

"Keep pumping," Peter told his sister, who had just started her turn on the ancient metal contraption. It looked something like an old farm water pump, only there was a hose attached to both ends. One hose sucked up the messy black bilge water inside the bottom of the boat, while the other hung over the side of the boat.

"It's stuck," replied Elise, giving the wood handle one more push.

"Here, let me try." Peter slid down next to where Elise was standing in the bottom of the boat, and she made room for him to work the pump.

But Peter couldn't move the handle any better than his sister. "Okay," he admitted. "I guess you're right."

Elise looked around for their uncle, who was returning from hauling a load down the dock.

"Uncle Morten," she called. "This pump is stuck."

"Doesn't surprise me with all the garbage floating in that water," he answered. "Here, just a minute." He pulled a screwdriver from his back pocket. "Probably something got sucked up inside."

Peter and Elise moved out of the way as their uncle unscrewed the pump's cover and carefully looked inside. He reached in to pull out a handful of something that looked like black paste held together with sticks and string.

"There's your problem," he declared, looking for a place to throw the mess.

"Wait a minute," said Elise, jumping down next to Uncle Morten. "Don't throw that out."

Uncle Morten hesitated, but Elise pointed at something in the black goo.

"There, see?" Elise pointed with a stick. "It's a cigar sticker. You know, the kind that goes around the outside."

Peter looked closer, and, sure enough, there was a crumpled and soggy cigar band in the middle of the string. "It says *Hirsch*. That's just the name of a cigar brand, isn't it?"

"It's a clue." Elise fished the paper ring out and held it high for everyone to see. "Uncle Morten doesn't smoke cigars. Right, Uncle Morten?"

Uncle Morten shook his head no.

"And has anyone smoked a cigar on your boat lately?"

Again their uncle shook his head. "Not on the *Anna Marie*."

"So it has to be connected to the fire," concluded Elise. "Maybe the person who set it was smoking the cigar—maybe he even used it to set the fire."

"I don't know, Elise," said Peter. "But if you're right, that's clue number two."

"Clue number two," repeated Elise, holding up her prize. She looked at it once more, then carefully set it aside on a dry corner of the deck. "Actually, clue number three, if you count the note."

By that time Grandfather Andersen had come limping down the ramp. He didn't move around as quickly as he used to, and Peter thought his grandfather always seemed out of breath. "Time for a break already?" Grandfather called over to them.

"Almost," answered Peter. "We're working."

Uncle Morten replaced the cover of the pump and Peter lowered himself back down to the inside of the boat. Like Elise, he was covered in black charcoal smudges.

"You look terrific," laughed his sister.

"Yeah," he replied. "So do you. It's the new style."

When it was Elise's turn to pump again, Peter looked around at the harbor. Like yesterday, ships were arriving with more Danish soldiers, but they were moving quickly off to the train station near the ferries. Still, the area was full of horn-tooting, flag-waving boats. The party had returned to the waterfront.

"Well," said Elise, pulling herself up out of the boat when she had finished pumping, "we already had our turn to wave flags. This is our way of celebrating."

"Why don't you two celebrate this pile of glass up to the garbage can?" asked their grandfather.

Elise stopped to pick up her cigar ring clue and put it carefully in her pocket. Then Peter followed her to the pier with a bucketful of broken glass. When they reached the boathouse, he noticed a small rolled-up piece of paper tucked into the crack of the door.

"What's this?" he asked Elise. "Not another note!"

"Here, let me see," said Elise, pulling out the note. "Yes, it's another one. This one says, 'Don't bother rebuilding,' and it's on the same notepaper as the first. Looks like the same handwriting, too."

" 'Don't bother rebuilding'? That's all it says?"

"Looks like it," answered Elise. "We better tell Uncle Morten and Grandfather."

As the twins turned back to the dock, Peter heard what sounded like a series of firecrackers, a pop-pop sound that jerked his head in the direction of the breakwater.

"Somebody's shooting!" shouted Peter, running down to the boat. "Hey! Somebody's shooting!"

Elise knew the sound as well as Peter. She ducked down to the deck of the third tug, only a few feet from the damaged *Anna Marie*.

"Over here, kids!" Peter's father yelled over the sound of more popping. Peter looked up to see him fly over the railing of the tug and scoop up a wide-eyed Elise under his arm. Uncle Morten was right behind him, helping Grandfather Andersen along.

They crouched under a deck railing, and Mr. Andersen yelled for Peter to keep down. But there was no need. Peter already had his face buried in the deck, his heart pumping with fear. He knew they weren't the target, but the shooting was too close for him to breathe easy.

There was another volley of shots, answered by different-sounding shots from the other side of the harbor. A moment later Peter was swept up by his father as they all sprinted back to the safety of the boathouse.

"Must be some Nazis holding out by those warehouses," said Uncle Morten as he peered out the window. Peter peeked out next to his uncle. All he could see were flashes coming out the side of a troop ship, and more flashes coming from the windows of a warehouse several hundred yards away.

"Don't they know the war is over?" asked Elise.

"They know," answered Grandfather Andersen. "They're just not giving up so easily."

"Come on," commanded Uncle Morten. "We're safe here, but we better get you kids home right away."

Uncle Morten hustled them all out the door of the boathouse and back out on the street. By that time, police cars with screaming sirens had pulled up to the waterfront to join in the battle. It was taking place farther out in the harbor area, but Uncle Morten wouldn't even let the kids look back.

"You two better stay away from the harbor for a day or two," warned Grandfather. "Your uncle or I will tell you when it's safe to come back."

"Does that mean we can't help fix up the boat?" asked Peter.

"Yes," answered Uncle Morten. "I mean no. There's plenty of time for that. We're not going to finish this thing overnight."

By that time the shooting had been going on for nearly fifteen minutes. Then there was a minute of silence. Peter tried to look out at the harbor between his uncle and grandfather. All he could see were police cars swarming toward the warehouse, and a minute later dozens of police officers disappeared inside.

Groups of people like themselves huddled close together, pointing. Then, almost as if nothing had happened, some music started again from a side street. Soldiers began stepping off one of the large ferries again.

"Did they get them?" Peter finally asked.

"Looks like it," replied his uncle. "The last shoot-out of the war is over. And this is not a sport for kids to watch!"

It hadn't seemed real, the gunfire had been so distant. But Peter couldn't help wondering who had been hiding in the warehouses, waiting for Danish troops to return home. *Maybe it was the guy I crashed into on the way home from church.* The thought gave Peter a chill.

Peter and Elise didn't wait for another scolding. Leaving Uncle Morten and their grandfather, they hurried up St. Anne's Street toward home—until Peter suddenly remembered.

"The note!" he cried, patting his pockets. "Elise, do you have it? With all the shooting, I totally forgot to tell Uncle Morten and Grandfather."

A woman passing by with her dog gave him an odd look.

"I have it," answered Elise. "Exhibit C." She waved the slip of paper in the air and turned around to run back to the harbor. "Two notes and a shoe now. We better tell them right away."

"Right," agreed Peter. As they ran back down to the boathouse, Peter tried to think again who might have left the threatening note.

"You know, Peter," Elise called out as she trotted along, "this really looks like a kid's handwriting, but I don't think it's Keld."

"I do."

"What if it's someone else?" persisted Elise. "Someone else who hates Uncle Morten because of the Underground or something?"

"That's just it," replied Peter. "Keld probably hates Uncle Morten because he got Keld's dad in trouble. You know what a terrible Nazi Mr. Poulsen was. I'll just bet you that when Uncle Morten escaped from Keld's dad—"

"Us too, remember."

"Yeah, us too. When we all escaped from Mr. Poulsen, don't

you think he got in trouble? He never came back to look for us."

"That was because the war was almost over."

Peter shook his head. "Uh-uh. I think he got in trouble, and now the Poulsens are out for revenge."

Peter thought for a moment as they neared the harbor for the second time that day. It wasn't fun to think back to the time when Keld's father had held them in a German prison after they had been caught helping an Underground newspaper. Peter shuddered.

"Could be," Elise finally admitted. "But I'm going to search for more clues before I decide."

"Fine. But I still think it's Keld."

6

FERRY FROM SWEDEN

"I'll get it!" Elise yelled when the phone rang late that Sunday evening. She collided with Peter in the hallway as he headed the same direction.

"Too late," replied their father in the kitchen. "I've already got it."

The twins listened from around the corner as their father answered questions.

"Yes, of course," he replied, sounding concerned. "No, I didn't know how serious it was . . . oh, I'm sorry to hear that. Yes . . . I think that would be good for him, too. Of course it wouldn't be a problem. We would be happy to. No, I'm sure she would feel the same. The twins will be thrilled, even though . . ."

"We will?" Peter looked at his sister and whispered, "What do you think we're going to be thrilled about?"

Elise put her finger to her lips. "Shh. Just listen."

"Okay, I've got a pencil," continued their father. "No, tomorrow night would be fine. It's a school night, but we can just run down to meet him at the ferry dock. Okay, arriving here in Helsingor at five-thirty-five. That's fine. We can take care of that later.

I hope your husband will be feeling better then."

Peter and Elise waited for their father to hang up the phone before they fired off their questions.

"Who do we have to pick up at the ferry?" added Peter.

"Hold it, hold it." Mr. Andersen held up his hands. "Let me get your mother in on this before I tell you the news. Karen?"

Mrs. Andersen was folding a towel as she came out from her room.

"Karen," Mr. Andersen told her, "that was Ruth Melchior, calling long-distance from Sweden. I could hardly hear her voice, it was so fuzzy."

"What did she say, Dad?" Peter asked impatiently.

Mr. Andersen held up his hand again.

"Hold on, Peter, and I'll tell you. Apparently they were getting ready to return home here to Denmark when just last night Mr. Melchior had another heart attack."

Mrs. Andersen put her hand to her mouth and gasped. "*Another* one? Oh dear, was it serious?"

"Sounds as if the doctors aren't quite sure yet, but I think it is. They say he can't be moved from the hospital. So while Ruth takes care of him, the Melchiors asked to have Henrik come here to stay with us for a few weeks."

"Henrik?" Peter asked, perking up. "Is that why you were talking about the ferry?"

"Right," answered his father. "It might be a while before Mr. Melchior is well enough to travel. They're putting Henrik on the ferry tomorrow afternoon."

Mr. Andersen looked at his wife. "I hope you don't mind—"

"Of course it's all right," agreed Mrs. Andersen. "Peter has plenty of space in his room. We can set up a cot."

"Sure!" Peter replied, his heart racing. "That'll be terrific. He can just come to school with us. I'll tell Mrs. Bernsted in class tomorrow." He ran over to Tiger's basket, where the cat watched every move he made.

"Did you hear that, Tiger? Henrik's coming back!"

"What time is it, Elise?"

This time Elise didn't look up from her book. "Peter, would you relax? If you really want to know what time it is, go sit in front of the kitchen clock. That's about the tenth time you've asked me since we got home from school."

Peter paced by the door to his sister's room. "Sorry," he mumbled.

"Peter, if you're looking for something to do," their mother called from the kitchen, "I have a whole pile of laundry to fold."

"I don't want to be late," answered Peter as he stepped into his sister's room and peeked out the window.

"That's fine, but don't pester your sister. And nobody's going to be late. We'll all walk over to the ferry dock when your father gets home from work. He should be here any minute."

"But what if he's late?"

Elise pretended to throw her book at him. "Peter!"

"Okay, okay." He retreated to his room and shut the door. "I just don't want to be late."

His school backpack sat untouched on top of Peter's small desk. He still had some math homework to do, and he knew he should probably work on the book report that was due later that week. But he couldn't keep his mind on schoolwork.

"I'm home!" Mr. Andersen whistled as he walked in the door of the apartment, the same way he always did at five-fifteen. The sound sent Peter flying off his bed and out to the front room.

"Dad!" cried Peter. "Where have you been? We don't want to be late."

"Where have I been?" Mr. Andersen laughed and looked at his wristwatch. "It's only five-fifteen."

"He's worried that we're not going to meet Henrik on time," said Elise, emerging from her room.

"Oh, right." Mr. Andersen looked at Peter. "No one's going to be late, Peter. Henrik's boat doesn't get in until five-thirty."

"But it's five-fifteen," insisted Peter. "Let's go!"

"All right, all right," Mrs. Andersen agreed from the kitchen. "I'm ready."

The ferry dock was only a ten-minute walk from their apartment, but Peter ran ahead of his sister and parents like an eager puppy.

"Wait for us!" called Elise. "The ferry's probably not even here yet."

But by that time Peter was around the corner, running past the big train terminal and into the station building next to where the ferries to Sweden docked.

Elise was right—the ferry wasn't there yet. When the others caught up, he was still standing in front of a waiting-room counter, hands on his hips.

"They're late," he declared. "It even says up on the arrival board that they're supposed to be here by now. But they're late."

"I wouldn't worry too much," Peter's father assured him, checking the large arrival board. "The ferries have been putting in some extra runs with all the people coming home. It'll be here."

But as ten minutes and then fifteen went by, Peter grew more fidgety. He paced the waiting room like an expectant father, looking out the window every half minute to see if the ferry was pulling into the harbor and up to the dock.

"What's keeping them?" he asked, pressing his nose against the window glass. He finally turned away after no one answered him.

Five minutes later the blunt end of an ocean-going ferry finally slipped into view.

"There!" Elise saw it first. "Here it comes!"

Peter sprang to the window to see the big vessel slowly come to a stop and bump into position between the twin sets of heavy pilings. Three deckhands looped their giant ropes to huge metal tie-up cleats on the waiting dock while ramps were lowered into place. It seemed to Peter that everything was moving in slow motion.

This ferry mainly carried train cars, which were pushed straight through the open front end. But soon people were coming down ramps with suitcases in their hands and eager smiles on their faces. Nearly everyone had someone waiting at the end of the ramp.

"Seems like we just did something like this," observed Mr. Andersen.

Peter's mother nodded. "A couple of days ago, when your brother came home."

"That's right." Mr. Andersen looked over a small sea of heads.

"Only this time it's not a surprise," added Peter, standing on his tiptoes.

The waiting room quickly became filled with shouting and hugging as dozens of people found their families. But still no Henrik.

"Are you sure this is the right boat?" Peter asked his father.

"It's the right boat, all right," answered Henrik, stepping out from behind a large woman with a wide-brimmed hat. He stood uncertainly in front of the Andersens, a small weekend bag in his right hand.

To Peter he looked almost the same as he had the night he and Elise had rowed him across to Sweden—tall, with much darker hair than Peter's and Elise's blond heads, a long ski-jump nose, and playful brown eyes.

"Henrik!" Peter almost jumped backward in surprise. "Where did you come from?"

"Hälsingfors," replied the tall boy. "It's not as big a city as Helsingor, but in Sweden . . ."

Just like Henrik, Peter thought. *The first thing he says when he gets back home is a joke.*

"Oh, Henrik," said Peter's mother, giving him a quick hug. "We're so glad you made it."

Peter stood back a little awkwardly with Elise while their dad took Henrik's bag. They tried to make their way through the crowd back out to the street.

"I guess the ferry was waiting for a train," explained Henrik. "It was full of soldiers, so they held up the boat. We had to sit at the dock in Sweden for almost half an hour."

"Well, Peter was going crazy waiting," reported Mr. Andersen.

As they walked down the street, Henrik put his arm around Peter's shoulder.

"So how was Sweden?" Peter asked. He couldn't think of anything else to say.

"It was okay," replied Henrik, looking around at the streets. "People talked funny and all, but it was okay. Are the pigeons all right?"

"They're great."

"Except we've hardly flown them since you left," added Elise.

Henrik looked at his friend. "Really? Why not?"

Peter shrugged. "It just didn't seem the same without you around to race them."

"Well," sighed Mrs. Andersen. "There are a lot of things you three will have to catch up on, aren't there?"

"Yes!" Henrik nodded. "Oh, and my mom said to tell you again how much we appreciate my being able to stay with you."

"Peter and Elise have been looking forward to it," answered Mrs. Andersen. "And Mr. Andersen talked with the young couple who have been taking care of your apartment. Everything is just fine, waiting for your family to get back. If there's anything you need to get out of your room, tell us."

Henrik smiled and pointed to his bag. "Everything I need is in there."

"We're very sorry to hear about your father," put in Mr. Andersen. "How is he?"

Henrik looked at the street, and his smile disappeared. Finally he shrugged his shoulders. "I'm not sure. I saw him in the hospital right after it happened. Yesterday they wouldn't let me in to see him at all. I didn't even get to say goodbye."

"Oh, Henrik," Elise said as they neared their apartment, "I'm so sorry."

Henrik gazed down at the cobblestone pavement and nodded. He looked back up as they began climbing the stairs to the Andersens' apartment, and the smile slowly returned.

"Hey, I remember this place," he said as he stepped up into the front room.

Mr. Andersen took Henrik's bag into Peter's room as Henrik looked out the windows.

"Good old Helsingor," he said quietly. "And no more Nazis."

"I guess not. But you know what?" Peter pulled Henrik aside. "Someone's trying to burn Uncle Morten's boat."

Henrik's eyes grew wide. "Burn it? What do you mean? While it's still in the water?"

"Yeah," Peter told him. "You should have been there. Maybe then the guy wouldn't have gotten away."

"What guy?"

"Keld Poulsen. I'm one hundred percent sure he set the fire."

"Peter," objected Elise. "We never actually saw Keld—or anyone else, really."

"Well, okay," replied Peter. "I'm ninety-nine percent sure. I saw Keld down at the harbor when all the boats were coming in. And the notes look as though a kid wrote them, remember?"

"Notes?" Henrik was trying to follow what the twins were telling him. Peter and Elise filled Henrik in on the details of the past Saturday's fire.

"That's incredible." Henrik whistled softly. "I thought the war was over."

"Not quite," said Elise. "And Tiger got run over, too."

"Tiger?" Henrik looked puzzled. "Is that the cat Uncle Morten told me about?"

"Yep," replied Peter. "He's a tough little animal."

"Is anyone hungry?" called Mrs. Andersen from the kitchen, interrupting the stories. "It's so late now you're probably all starving. Especially the world traveler."

"I sure am," agreed Henrik, following the twins to the kitchen. "I almost had to eat the Swedish chocolate bars my mom gave me to give you."

"Chocolate?" Peter rubbed his hands together.

"After dinner," warned their mother. "Oh, but chocolate does sound wonderful."

"We'll tell you more about the fire after dinner," Peter whispered to Henrik as they bent down on the floor next to Tiger's basket. "But here's Tiger with his broken leg."

"Hey, Tiger." Henrik scratched the cat behind his ears, and Tiger began to purr. "I broke my arm once, did you know that, little fella?"

"He purrs a lot," said Elise.

"Wash up now," Mrs. Andersen reminded them.

"We're going to find out who set the fire," Peter told his friend as they washed their hands. "And I'll bet you anything it was Keld."

CINDERELLA'S SLIPPER

"Come on, Henrik," Peter yelled into the crowd of kids surrounding Henrik in the school hallway. "You're going to be late on your first day back at school."

Peter couldn't blame his friend. All the other kids wanted to hear the whole story—and Henrik didn't mind being the star. In fact, the second day of classes after the war ended turned out to be Henrik Melchior Day at Helsingor Public School Number Twelve.

During a special assembly that Tuesday morning, Mr. Jensen, the principal, called Henrik up to the front for a special pat on the back as everyone clapped. Then there was a special song time and celebration, and everyone got to wave little Danish flags again. The teachers were all smiling and singing along, too.

Back in the classroom, it was almost the same—Henrik was the center of attention, at least for that morning.

"Henrik," said Mrs. Bernsted, the teacher. She sat up straight in her chair. Peter always thought everything about her looked straight, from her face to the way she stood in front of the blackboard with her long, straight pointer. But she was a fair teacher, and there were times when she even laughed a little. "Tell us your favorite part about living in Sweden for the past year and a half."

Henrik stood at the front of the class, obviously enjoying himself.

"Swedish chocolate," he replied, and everyone laughed.

Annelise Kastrup raised her hand. "What was school like?"

"Kind of like here, except we didn't have enough books for each of us to have our own. They put all the Danish kids together, and one teacher had to teach three or four grades."

Peter sat back, watching his friend answer questions. Henrik was like a comedian, making little jokes, keeping people laughing.

"When is your family coming home?" asked Ruth Glensvig from the front row.

The smile disappeared from Henrik's face, and he mumbled something that sounded like "I don't know." Then he turned to Mrs. Bernsted. "Can I sit down now?"

"What?" asked Mrs. Bernsted, looking surprised. "Well, yes, of course. Thank you for sharing with us."

At lunch, Henrik was again the center of attention, but no one asked about his father or his family.

"Really, I don't know why everyone's making such a fuss about me coming back," he told Peter, his mouth full of cheese. "It's not such a big deal."

"Sure it is," replied Peter. "It's big news."

"I suppose. But you know, you guys had all the excitement over here while I was gone. All I really did in Sweden was go to the Danish school. Until my Dad got sick."

Peter studied his sandwich. "I hope he gets better soon, Henrik."

"Yeah, me too." Henrik rubbed his eyes quickly, then looked around at the lunch crowd and wrinkled his forehead. "What happened to Keld Poulsen?"

Peter shrugged. "Absent today, I think. You're disappointed he's not here?"

"It's just that if Keld isn't here, we can't compare the old shoe Elise found to his foot."

"Oh, sure. You suppose Keld would want to try it on for us? We could tell him where we found it and everything."

"No, that's not what I mean. I just think there must be some way we can get another one of his shoes so we can see if they're the same size."

Peter fidgeted on the bench. Even though he still thought Keld was responsible for the fire, part of him just wanted to forget the whole thing. "Yeah, but even if we could get ahold of one of his shoes, it wouldn't prove anything. Lots of people fit in the same size shoe."

"You're hard to figure, Peter." Henrik stood up. "I thought maybe you or Elise would have some kind of plan. We've got to start somewhere, don't you think? Otherwise, whoever set the fire could do it again."

Then Henrik caught sight of Elise chatting with a couple of her friends. "Hey, Elise!" he yelled.

She looked up and waited for the boys to walk over. Her friends had drifted off by the time Henrik and Peter walked up, leaving the three of them alone by the two garbage cans where students threw away their wax-paper wrappers and apple cores.

"Elise," Henrik lowered his voice. "Do you still have the shoe?"

Elise nodded. "Yes, it's at home."

"Good," replied Henrik. "Because I have a plan."

"You do?" Peter hoped it wasn't anything like Henrik's earlier idea.

"Yeah," replied Henrik. "All we have to do is slip a piece of paper under Keld's foot. Then we trace it and compare it to the shoe Elise found."

"That's not a plan," commented Elise. "That's a way to get yourself hurt. It would be simpler to go to his house, walk into his room, pick out a shoe, and make a tracing. Or maybe just hold up the shoe I found next to another one. We'll see if it matches what we have already."

"We?" asked Peter, "Who do you mean by *we*?"

"You and Henrik, that's who I mean," she answered with a smile. "I'd go myself, but Keld would never let me in."

"What makes you think we'll have any better luck?" asked Peter.

"Well," she replied, "I figured out the hard part. You boys just have to make it happen."

"Yeah," agreed Henrik, nodding swiftly. "Maybe we'll even find the other shoe." He grabbed Peter's arm and marched him toward the door of the lunchroom as the bell rang for class. "Leave it to us, Elise. I know how we can pull it off."

Peter crumpled his lunch sack and threw it as hard as he could toward the trash can by the door. He missed. One way or another, they were heading for trouble again. He was sure of it.

"I was just kidding, Peter," Elise leaned in to Peter and whispered as they left. "You're not really going to do it, are you?"

———————

Henrik wouldn't explain his plan the rest of the afternoon, and Peter didn't have a chance to talk to him during science or language. By that time, Peter had decided he would refuse to go along if Henrik suggested storming Keld Poulsen's apartment. *I just won't do it*, Peter told himself.

Finally, with five minutes of school left, Peter scribbled out a three-word note and dropped it on Henrik's desk as he walked by to collect books.

What's the plan?

Henrik just smiled and held the note in his fist. When the bell rang, he slipped out of his seat to stand in front of Mrs. Bernsted's desk. The teacher looked up from her grade book over her thick, black-rimmed glasses at the tall boy.

"Well, Henrik." Mrs. Bernsted cleared her throat and straightened her back. "As I'm sure everyone has said a hundred times, we're all very glad you made it back."

Henrik smiled politely and rocked on his heels. "Yes, ma'am. I'm glad to be back too."

At his desk, Peter shuffled the day's homework into his knap-sack, wondering what Henrik was up to. He tried not to stare. Everyone else had left the classroom by then, except Ruth Glens-vig, who was sharpening her pencils by the window.

"Mrs. Bernsted?" asked Henrik, shifting from one foot to the other.

"Yes, Henrik?"

"I was wondering about Keld."

"Keld?" Mrs. Bernsted looked puzzled. Peter closed his eyes and leaned back in his chair, afraid of what he might hear next.

"Sure," answered Henrik. "Peter and I were going to stop by his apartment on the way home from school today, and, well, I just thought we should bring him his homework so he doesn't get behind."

Mrs. Bernsted studied Henrik's expression for a moment, then looked down at her grade book. Peter fell over backward and crashed into the desk behind him.

"Peter!" called the teacher. "You're too old for that kind of nonsense. Are you all right?"

Red in the face, Peter scrambled to his feet and straightened out the desk and chair. "I'm sorry, Mrs. Bernsted. I'm fine."

The edge of the desk had caught him just behind his right ear, though, and Peter thought he felt a goose egg coming on as he rubbed his head. But Mrs. Bernsted turned back to Henrik.

"Well, actually, Henrik," she continued, "that would be a fine idea. Are you sure?"

"It's really no trouble," Henrik assured her.

Peter wished he had left at the bell with everyone else. *Henrik's really flipped*, he thought as the two boys hurried outside.

"Are you nuts, Henrik?" Peter raised his voice a notch. "What were you talking about in there? It sounds pretty sneaky."

"It's not sneaky," explained Henrik. "We have to get into

Keld's house to find the other shoe. But we don't want to accuse someone who really didn't do it, do we?"

"No, I guess not."

"So we have to find out for sure. This is the best way." Henrik twirled around a lightpost like a gymnast.

"Right," replied Peter, still reluctant. "He'll beat us into the pavement when we show up. He's a maniac, just like his dad. We don't even know for sure where the apartment is—"

"We do too." replied Henrik. "Right over on the corner of Ferry Street."

Both boys knew the neighborhood—an area of taverns and older row houses located near the train station, not far from the harbor. It wasn't a part of town they liked to spend time in, but it took only ten minutes to walk there from school.

"But first," said Henrik as they passed Peter's street, "we have to run in and get the shoe."

"That's what I was afraid of," replied Peter, making the turn.

Peter tiptoed up his stairs while Henrik waited outside.

"Hurry up!" Henrik called up from the sidewalk. Peter wasn't sure why they should hurry, but he whisked through the front door and down the hall, trying not to make a sound. When he reached his sister's room, he quietly slid open the closet door and groped around on the floor for the lone shoe.

"Looking for this?" asked Elise, standing in the doorway. She held the shoe in her hand.

"Oh! There it is. We just need it for a few minutes."

"I told you I was kidding about that idea," she warned him. "If Keld is the one behind the fire, he's going to figure out what we're up to. He's not exactly Cinderella, you know."

"We'll be careful," replied Peter. "Henrik says he has a plan."

Elise frowned, then tossed the shoe to Peter. "That's what I was afraid of. I should come along."

"Yeah, but you said yourself that Keld would be even more suspicious if three of us showed up at his door." Peter pulled off his school backpack and stuffed the shoe inside as he backed out of his sister's room—right into his mother.

"Oh, sorry, Mom," he said, startled. "I was just going out."

"Any schoolwork, Peter?"

"Only a little," Peter replied. "We'll be back in a little while. Henrik promised Mrs. Bernsted that we'd drop off some homework for someone who was absent today."

After a quick check on Tiger, Peter was out the door and down the steps before he had to answer any more questions. Henrik was waiting in front of Illemann's Bakery, looking hungry.

"You're slow," said Henrik as Peter trotted up to the bread-filled window. "I was about to have a snack." The smell reached out to Peter, too.

"Let's get this over with."

Henrik nodded and tore himself away from the window. "Okay. I guess we can eat later. Here's the plan. . . ."

Keld Poulsen lived with his mother in a small flat above a particularly seedy-looking drinking place. At least the view of the ships in the harbor was nice—but all the shades in the Poulsens' windows were drawn.

"Right there." Henrik nodded at the number on a black door. "Fifty-two Ferry Street. Now remember, we *both* need to go in. One person might need to distract Keld while the other one checks for the shoe. Are you scared?"

"I'm not scared. But what if Keld's sick in bed?"

"I'll bet he's not sick. He's either faking it, or he just stayed home from school."

A train was just coming in from Copenhagen on its way to the ferries, where it would roll onto a ship bound for Sweden.

"So do you remember what to do?" Henrik shouted above the noise of grinding train wheels and engines. The trains made a mighty clanking sound as they coupled a few more cars, and the boys stood uncertainly in front of a door with peeling black paint.

Peter frowned, but he felt in his pack for the shoe and nodded.

Then he sighed and rapped on the door three times, hoping that no one was home.

"See?" Peter turned to his friend. "No one home." But the doorknob slowly turned, and suddenly Keld Poulsen stood before them in his doorway. The big boy stood blinking at them, looking as surprised as Peter was scared. He was wearing a worn plaid bathrobe that was several sizes too large. A scarf was wrapped around his neck. Peter had to take a step backward as the foul smell of stale cigarette smoke hit him.

"What do *you* want?" The question came out with a sneer.

"Brought your homework, Keld," volunteered Henrik with a broad smile. *Too broad,* thought Peter. "I just got back from Sweden. Thought you might need it."

"You were gone? I didn't notice," Keld taunted him. He looked skeptically at the pile of books Henrik still cradled under his arm and scratched his head. His dirty blond hair seemed to stick out in every direction.

Henrik ignored the jab and held up a math book for Keld to see. "Math, see? Mrs. B said it would be a good idea. Thought you might need it."

Keld just stood there in the doorway, squinting at Henrik and Peter as though they were visitors from space. He started to step back, as if to slam the door in their faces. Peter wondered if they shouldn't turn and run while they had a chance. But Henrik stepped forward and put his foot in the door.

"Don't forget your homework, Keld."

As Keld tried to close the door, Peter felt a leftover flash of hot anger—the same kind he had always felt before for the Germans. Only this time, it made him clench his fists and grit his teeth at Keld.

Keld, the one who had always gotten them into so much trouble. Keld, the bully who had wanted to be a Nazi. Keld, the one who was probably trying to burn up Uncle Morten's boat—and now was trying to hide. Standing there in his ridiculous bathrobe, Keld looked more helpless than Peter could remember. For a brief second, Peter wanted to push Keld aside, march into the dingy apartment, and search for the other shoe. It had to be here.

You did it! Peter wanted to shout. *You hurt us! You put my sister and me in that stupid prison. You tried to burn up my uncle's boat. You can't get away with it anymore, and now you're going to pay!*

Instead a woman's voice shrieked from just behind Keld. Peter winced; it reminded him too much of fingernails screeching across a chalkboard.

"Keld, dear, who's at the door?"

Henrik pulled his foot back, and the train rumbling finally stopped.

"Just a couple of kids from school, Mom. They're leaving—"

"Well, don't just stand there talking in the doorway," she interrupted. "Where are your manners? Have your friends come in."

"Uh, they were just leaving, Mom," stammered Keld. He reached out to grab his pile of books, but Henrik held them tightly.

"Thanks, Mrs. Poulsen," Henrik called into the house.

Peter tried to hide behind Henrik as they slipped by Keld and stepped into the small front hallway.

"What do you think you're doing?" Keld whispered hoarsely.

Peter didn't answer, just shivered. He was over his flash of anger. Now he was inside Keld Poulsen's apartment.

"Oh, how nice," bubbled Mrs. Poulsen. She was a large woman, with her hair pulled up on top of her head in a bun. Like Keld, she wore a bathrobe and slippers, only hers were pink. She showed her large teeth between made-up red lips as she saw Henrik and Peter walk in. "Such nice friends to visit Keld."

"Uh, we brought his homework, Mrs. Poulsen." Henrik held out Keld's books and presented them to him.

"Oh!" Mrs. Poulsen smiled. "That's so thoughtful of you boys. Goodness knows he needs his homework. I would have fetched it myself, but I didn't want to leave poor Keld here alone. Especially not with his sore throat. Right, Keld?"

Keld just nodded sullenly.

Peter hardly listened as he worried about what they had come to do. He wondered how he would find one of Keld's shoes without being seen. And there was a nagging thought in the back of his head. He hadn't ever done anything quite this sneaky before.

"Let me show you what you have to do, Keld," Henrik volunteered. By then Peter was sweating nervously.

"Oh, that's a good idea," bubbled Mrs. Poulsen. She led them through the tiny front sitting room into an even tinier kitchen.

Keld still seemed as if he were in a daze, but he sat down at the kitchen table. Their only light was a bare light bulb hanging several feet above the table. After she gave her son's book a quick glance, Keld's mother disappeared down a dark hall leading out of the kitchen, away from the front room.

Where do I find a shoe? Peter wondered. He stood by the table and shifted his weight from foot to foot while Henrik cheerfully explained the math, science, and language assignments. When Peter looked down at the boy's feet, he saw Keld was wearing big blue slippers.

"Listen," said Keld, after he had checked to see that his mother was out of sight. "I don't need your lousy homework. And you can just play your stupid teacher games somewhere else." He stood up, slamming the math book shut.

"Hey, that's fine." Henrik stood up as well. "We're just trying to do you a favor."

Keld was steaming. "I told you, I don't need your favors."

Peter was ready to run out, but Keld almost shoved the two boys back through the sitting room toward the door. Then Peter saw a small doormat piled carefully with shoes just inside the front door. Why hadn't he seen it before? Two pairs obviously belonged to Mrs. Poulsen, but one looked like a pair of boy's— or men's—street shoes! If he could just look to see how big they were and compare them to the shoe they already had . . .

"Oh, Keld," Mrs. Poulsen called from the kitchen. "Are your friends leaving so soon?"

"Yeah, Mom," he called back. "They have to leave."

"Well, don't let them go before they have a snack. Come back here right now and we'll give them a piece of bread and cheese. I'm having some myself."

"I really think they have to go, Mom," said Keld, opening the front door.

"That sounds great, Mrs. Poulsen," said Henrik, breaking free of Keld and slipping back toward the kitchen.

Keld stood there looking back and forth from Henrik to Peter. Finally he grunted in disgust and followed Henrik, leaving Peter alone for a moment in the entry.

This is my chance, thought Peter. As soon as Keld turned his back, Peter fell to his knees and unbuttoned his backpack. He fished around for the shoe, and had just pulled it out when he heard someone walking toward him. There wasn't time to do anything but quickly stuff the shoe back in and turn around.

"Hey, what are you doing?" asked Keld. He had reappeared at the entry to the living room with Henrik peeking nervously over his shoulder.

Peter looked up with wide eyes, wondering if Keld had seen him with the shoe in his hand. *Maybe not,* Peter guessed.

"What am I doing?" Peter quickly gathered his papers and books off the floor and stuffed them back into his bag. He stood up and felt for the doorknob. "Just getting my things together. I'm not hungry."

"Hey, well, have fun with the homework, Keld," Henrik told the big boy as he stuffed a piece of French bread into his mouth. Then he looked back at the kitchen. "And thanks for the bread, Mrs. Poulsen. But we really do have to be going."

"Isn't your friend going to have a slice?" asked Mrs. Poulsen. "There's plenty left."

"He's not hungry," explained Henrik.

"Yeah," agreed Peter, pulling open the door. "We do have to be going."

"Thank you so much for visiting," came Mrs. Poulsen's voice, almost sickly sweet. She appeared and stood with her hands tightly clamped on Keld's shoulder. "It was so thoughtful for you to think of him. He should be back in school again tomorrow, right, dear?"

Keld's icy expression was enough to quicken Peter's rush out the door. "I'm not sure, Mom," he whined. "I think I'm feeling a little hot again."

"Well, then maybe you should be going back to bed, Keld," said Mrs. Poulsen. "I thought you were feeling better, but maybe the visit was too much. . . ."

Peter didn't wait for Henrik, he turned around and half trotted, half ran down the sidewalk in the direction of home. *The visit was too much, all right—for me,* he thought, dusting off his hands.

"So, did you see the shoes?" Henrik ran up behind Peter like an eager puppy nipping at his heels. Another long, noisy train was bumping its way down the tracks, making as much noise as ever. Peter was just glad to get away from Keld's apartment.

"I saw some shoes," replied Peter, fishing the shoe out of his pack once more and tossing it to Henrik. "But I think Keld saw me trying to pull the old shoe out of my pack. I didn't have a chance to do anything."

Henrik turned the shoe over in his hands while Peter kept walking as fast as he could through the late afternoon bicycle crowd. Henrik trotted next to him to keep up.

"I tried to keep him back in the kitchen for another minute," said Henrik. "It was a good try."

Peter said nothing.

"It was a good try," Henrik repeated. "We'll just have to try again."

"Uh-uh," answered Peter, shaking his head. "I'm not going back to his house ever again."

"Okay, maybe not. So we'll find another way."

Again, Peter didn't answer. He tried to think about something else—anything other than Keld Poulsen, the fire, or the shoe.

8

THE DAY THE BANANAS RETURNED

"Now I'm sure the war is over." Elise sniffed the air on the way home from school the next Friday afternoon.

"Of course it is," said Peter, keeping up with her and Henrik. "We've been waving flags all week."

"And the British are here," added Henrik, waving to a jeepload of British soldiers. The Danish people loved them with their jaunty caps and friendly smiles. They were a sign of the liberation of Denmark.

The Germans were gone, too. There hadn't been any shooting since that Sunday afternoon a week earlier, and Peter had tried not to think about their visit to Keld Poulsen's apartment. Besides, nothing else had happened to their uncle's fishing boat, and work was coming along on the new wheelhouse. People were starting to smile and laugh again—even their parents.

"No, I don't mean those things," Elise insisted. "I mean, now I can really tell. Just look."

Elise pointed down the street to where a crowd of people had neatly lined up on the sidewalk outside a green grocer's shop.

"What's the deal?" asked Henrik. "Why is everyone in line for cabbages?"

Even as they watched, more people were running to get in line. It was the same store where they had often been sent by their mother during the war with ration cards to buy what few vegetables they were allowed: small cabbages, green cabbages, red cabbages, beets, or potatoes. That was about all there had been—but there had never been a line like the one they were now looking at.

"Not cabbages, silly," answered Elise with a smile. "Bananas."

"Bananas?" Peter asked. "How can you tell?"

"I can smell them," said Elise. She pretended to have a banana in her hand, made a peeling motion, then popped the pretend fruit into her mouth. "And they're delicious!"

"No way," said Henrik, his eyes following the crowd. "I haven't seen a banana since I was little." He meant before the war.

"I think I remember what they tasted like," said Peter, closing his eyes. "Sweet and like . . ."

Henrik started running down the street toward the line-up, and Peter yelled after him.

"Where are you going?"

"You guys can stand there eating your pretend bananas. I'm going to see if we can get the real thing before they're gone."

"Wait a minute," Peter yelled back. "I'm coming too."

By the time the twins and Henrik joined the line, there were at least thirty people in front of them. They were sandwiched between a large older woman with a big sack and a tall woman—probably about Mrs. Andersen's age—with a short little dachshund on a leash. Peter thought the tall woman looked familiar. Maybe she was a friend of his mother's, but he was too shy to ask.

"You're not going to spend all the money your mom sent you on bananas, are you?" Peter asked Henrik. He looked nervously at the wiener dog, who was sniffing his leg.

"Of course not," answered Henrik. "Just a taste."

Peter bent down to pet the dog, but the animal jumped back and showed his teeth with a throaty little growl.

"Bruno!" the woman scolded her dog. "Shame on you."

But Bruno did not seem to hear his master. Before Peter could pull his hand away, the dog snapped at him.

"Yeow!" he cried. Henrik and Elise jumped back at the same time.

"I'm terribly sorry," apologized the woman, yanking on the dog's leash. "He's usually very friendly. Are you all right?"

"Missed me," declared Peter, checking his hand to make sure. Bruno licked his lips and choked from his tightened collar. For the next ten minutes in line, the three kept as far away from the dachshund as they could.

"Next," said the grocer, and they stepped up to the counter. The grocer, Mr. Mogensen, gave the kids a knowing look. "You'll be wanting some bananas, will you? These are the first ones from South America since the war ended."

"Yes, sir," replied Henrik. "How many can I get for this?" He held up a yellow coin.

The grocer smiled and held out two bananas, exchanging them for Henrik's money. They were still half green and had black splotches, but to Peter they looked terrific.

"Thanks!" Henrik held up the fruit like a prize and headed for the door, followed by Peter and Elise. On the way out the door, there was a yip and a snarl. Peter jumped, realizing he had just stepped on Bruno's foot.

"Sorry!" he apologized, dashing out to the street.

All this excitement over bananas, he thought.

"So, do you want a bite?" asked Henrik, heading down the street toward the harbor. He held out one of the bananas, which he had halfway peeled. Peter and Elise each took a careful nibble, then smiled.

"Take a bite, not a nibble," insisted Henrik.

"Now I remember what they taste like," said Peter, taking a bigger bite. He closed his eyes for a moment and tried to remember all the other things they hadn't been able to eat during the war, but the memories were fuzzy.

"Yeah," echoed Elise. "Pretty good after five years of potatoes and cabbage."

As they walked down St. Anne's Street toward the harbor, Peter noticed a cluster of four teenagers huddled just off the main street. He tried not to stare, but a cloud of smoke rose from the group, and they were laughing.

"Don't look now," whispered Elise. "But I think I see Keld in that group."

Out of the corner of his eye, Peter noticed him, too. Keld was in the middle of the huddle, surrounded by smoke. Even from across the street, Peter could hear the boy's coughs. Then one of the teenagers stepped aside, and their eyes met for a second. Keld took the bulging cigar out of his mouth, looked away, and handed it to someone else.

"Did you see that?" asked Elise out of the corner of her mouth. They walked faster, past Henrik.

"See what?" Henrik tossed his remaining banana into the air, catching it behind his back.

"Keld Poulsen," Peter hissed. "Back there in the alley."

Henrik looked over his shoulder and studied the group of teens for a moment.

"I don't see him."

"He was back there in the middle of all those older teenage guys," Elise remarked. "Smoking a cigar."

"Yech," declared Henrik as they continued walking down to the harbor. "Well, he can keep it."

When they stepped into Grandfather Andersen's boathouse, Henrik spoke again. "Speaking of Keld, are we giving up on the whole detective thing?"

Peter walked over to the chicken wire that divided Grandfather's work area from the pigeon coop. He had been afraid Henrik would say something like that.

"Maybe we should fly the birds again," said Peter, hoping to change the subject. "We haven't done that for months."

As if he had understood, Peter's pigeon fluttered in a brief circle around the coop, sending feathers flying.

"I'm ready for a race." Henrik stood up and launched his banana peel into a trash barrel next to Grandfather Andersen's workbench. "But what about the notes? And your uncle's boat?"

Peter took a deep breath.

"Henrik's right," said Elise. "We still need to find out who wrote the notes. And who the shoe belongs to. If we don't, nobody else will. You still have the notes, don't you?"

Peter nodded. While Henrik put his second banana down carefully on a corner of the workbench, Peter dug through his pockets, found the two notes, and unfolded them carefully so everyone could see.

"Okay, look," said Henrik. "Maybe we can find out something else just by looking at the notes. Maybe there's a clue in them."

"I've looked at them, Henrik," sighed Peter. "Why would there be a clue? The only thing we know for sure is that they're from a kid with terrible handwriting."

Elise bent over the notes again, studying the messages.

"Lots of adults have terrible handwriting," she noted.

"Not like this," countered Peter. "This note looks like my writing when I try to write with my left hand."

Henrik picked up a thick carpenter's pencil from the workbench and tried to copy the writing of the notes using his left hand to write and the side of a board as a tablet.

"Hey, look," he said, holding the note and the piece of wood closer together. "They almost look the same."

Peter looked at Henrik's work and tilted his head. There were some similarities, but it was hard to say.

"Well, one thing's for sure," Peter finally concluded.

"What's that?" Henrik sounded curious.

"You didn't write the notes."

Henrik threw the notepaper at Peter. "Thanks for that brilliant tip."

Elise didn't look up, only picked up the note and studied it more closely.

"Come on, you guys," she said quietly. "This is serious."

"Okay, sorry." Henrik tried to flatten the folds of the note while Elise stared at the paper.

" 'When Morten returns, he burns,' " she reread the first one.

"And that's already happened," sighed Peter. "At least, his boat has burned."

"But then there's the other note." Henrik jabbed the crumpled piece of paper with his finger. "I think 'Don't bother rebuilding' means he's going to come back and set another fire."

"Probably," agreed Peter. "But what about the cigar ring and the shoe? Don't you think if it were really serious, Uncle Morten would be trying to find out more about it? He just tells us not to worry, that it's some kind of prank."

"Well, I don't think it's a kid's prank," said Elise. "And now the cigar ring has given us another clue." She held up one of the notes up to the bright sunshine beaming in the window.

Peter sat down on an old can of paint. "I thought you'd say that. So if the fire was set by someone smoking a Hirsch cigar, and we saw Keld Poulsen smoking a cigar, then it must have been Keld who set the fire—right?"

"Not quite," she replied. "Even though it makes sense, that's only one possibility. It could have been set by someone else who was smoking a cigar. Maybe one of the teenagers. Or it could have been someone else we don't even know about."

Henrik groaned. "You're just making it complicated, Elise."

"No, I'm not," she answered. "We have to look at all the possibilities."

"Okay," continued Henrik. "But which one do you think it is?"

Elise spun around to face the boys, her finger pointing at the ceiling. "I don't think it was Keld. That's too easy. Keld hates us, his father hates us. But that doesn't automatically mean he did it."

"That still sounds good to me," Peter disagreed.

"No," argued Elise. "I don't know who it is yet, but right now I think it was one of the people Keld was hanging around with. They didn't look too nice, you know."

Henrik nodded. "I think Elise may be right. Those guys were pretty rough looking."

"But we still don't know for sure," put in Peter.

Henrik looked at him. "I thought you were one hundred percent sure it was Keld before. Now you don't sound so sure."

"Well," Peter defended himself. "I still think it's him. At least ninety-nine percent of me does."

Elise paced the floor impatiently. "We're just going in circles with this. We need some better clues."

"What about the shoe?" asked Henrik.

"I've been thinking about that." Elise seemed lost in thought. "It's too big for Keld, even if he does have big feet. And have you ever seen him wear a shoe like that? It's a loafer, the kind adults wear."

Peter still wasn't too sure of his sister's conclusions, even though they sounded good. "Why didn't you tell us that before?"

"I didn't think of it before."

Henrik clapped his fist in his hand. "Elise is right. These clues aren't getting us anywhere. There has to be a way for us to find out more."

"Right," agreed Elise. "They could burn the boat down tonight, and we would still be standing in here, scratching our heads."

Everyone jumped when the door flew open. A long wooden beam came through the opening, followed by Uncle Morten. Elise hopped up to help her uncle with the load.

"Well, look who's here," announced Uncle Morten. "Did I hear someone say they're just standing around? I could use some help cutting this lumber."

Henrik looked at the twins and raised his eyebrows. "Well, at least no one will try anything funny with the boat while we're here, right?"

Peter and Elise nodded.

"So put us to work, Uncle Morten." Elise helped her uncle set his load down on the floor. "Do you need us to help you get the *Anna Marie* pulled up on land so we can clean it up?"

"No, not yet." Uncle Morten clapped the sawdust off his hands and pointed out the window at the next boatyard, barely visible past a couple of warehouses. "Some other boat is using the hoist today. We get it tomorrow. But I could still use some help this afternoon."

As if they had planned their routine, Peter and Henrik pulled back their shirtsleeves and flexed their muscles at each other.

"So, Uncle Morten," growled Peter in his most gravelly voice. "Which one of the muscle men do you want to help you?"

Uncle Morten played along and bent down to examine the boys' arms. As if he were choosing grapefruit at the market, he squeezed first Henrik's arm, then Peter's. Both boys grunted, then held their breath until their faces turned red.

"Hmm, tough choice," he said, standing back and pulling his sandy-colored beard. "But I think I'll have to choose Elise. She's a little more dependable."

"Aww, no fair," moaned Peter. Elise just smiled and stuck out her chin at the boys.

"What's not fair?" Uncle Morten opened the door and pointed down at the boat. "Boys, go down to the boat, would you please, and help Grandfather hold things steady. We're putting up ceiling beams."

Down at the boat, Peter and Henrik hopped up to the sawdust-covered deck. During the past week, they had already pulled off all the burned wood. Uncle Morten and Grandfather Andersen had been working hard, and the new deckhouse was quickly taking shape.

"Looks like it's almost all framed in, Grandfather," observed Peter.

"Almost," replied Grandfather Andersen. It wasn't hot, but he mopped his forehead with his handkerchief. Then he coughed, and Peter winced at the hacking sound.

"Are you okay?" he asked.

"I'm fine. Right now, boys, I just want one of you to hold the end of this beam while I measure it. Henrik, you're the tall one. And Peter, why don't you grab the pencil over there."

Peter followed his grandfather's instructions, and they measured a series of five beams to go across the top and hold up the slightly rounded roof.

Henrik looked out over the water while they were holding up another beam. "Good thing those idiots aren't shooting at us anymore."

"Yeah," agreed Peter. "Idiots."

Grandfather Andersen looked up from where he was marking one end of a board.

"The war's over, Peter," he said quietly, looking his grandson in the eye. His expression was soft, almost sad. "There are no idiots anymore. We don't call anyone an idiot."

"I just . . . I just meant I'm glad the Germans are gone," gulped Peter. Grandfather's words had caught him off guard.

Henrik backed up a step, too, as if he was afraid that Peter's grandfather would be talking at him. Peter supposed the message had been meant as much for Henrik as for him, but he had never heard his grandfather scold Henrik directly.

"Everyone's glad the Germans are gone, Peter," continued Grandfather. "But you can stop calling people idiots, or anything like that. Understand? It's time to let go of your anger."

Peter just nodded and looked down.

First Elise, and now Grandfather. He understood what his grandfather was trying to tell him, but he wasn't sure he wanted to hear it. "Yes, sir," he mumbled.

What he really wanted to do was jump up and shout something like "I'm never going to forgive the Germans!" He thought about what would happen if he did, though, and kept silent. After what seemed like a long silence, Peter's grandfather went back to his measuring and figuring. At the end of each beam, he drilled a hole with his hand drill.

"Let go, Peter," came his grandfather's voice, as if in the background somewhere. "I said, you can let go of the beam now."

Peter looked down at his knuckles, white from gripping a beam his grandfather had been trying to set up. Only then did he realize he had been daydreaming.

"What? Oh . . . sure." Peter eased the beam down and loosened his grip.

"Thank you." Grandfather Andersen took out his tape measure. "You looked as if you were getting pretty attached to that piece of wood. Are you all right?"

"Sure." Peter nodded his head and tried to look normal. He was afraid his grandfather would say something else, so he turned his attention to helping Henrik pick up another piece of the roof. Grandfather gave him a questioning look, but no one said anything more.

Five minutes of tense silence later, Uncle Morten and Elise returned to the boat with an armload of smaller boards. Elise was giggling about something funny her uncle had just said.

"We're back," announced Uncle Morten, laying down his load in the middle of the boat. "Does someone want to help me put these frames up. Henrik?"

"Sure."

"All we need are a couple more tools I left up on the workbench. We'll need a plane and that big red-handled file."

"Plane and file," repeated Henrik.

"File and plane," said Peter.

The two boys ran up the steep dock ramp to the boathouse, racing each other as they went. Henrik was the first through the door.

"What are you looking for?" asked Peter. "The plane and the file are right there in front of you."

"Yeah, I know that," replied Henrik, sounding suspicious. "I was just looking around for my other banana." He pointed at a cleared-off corner of the worktable. "I left it right there. You didn't snitch it, did you?"

Peter shook his head. "No way. Not me. Maybe Uncle Morten . . . no, he wouldn't do that. And the pigeons, they don't like bananas."

Peter looked over at the birds. Number Two, his homing pigeon, just stared back at them with his round, orange eyes.

"So who took the banana, huh?" Peter asked his bird.

Henrik opened up the door and hollered down at the dock where the *Anna Marie* was tied up. "Did any of you steal the banana I brought for a snack?"

Peter looked over Henrik's shoulder to see Uncle Morten throw up his hands. "I noticed it up there on the workbench," he shouted back. "We were tempted, but we didn't touch it, Henrik."

Henrik looked back at the workbench. "That's strange. You've been with me the whole time, and they say they never touched it."

"Maybe you left it somewhere else," suggested Peter, checking some shelves next to the workbench. No fruit.

"No, I left it here." Henrik pointed once more to the spot on the workbench. Then he poked his head outside again. "It had to be—Peter, come here."

Peter followed his friend outside to where Henrik had walked over to the side of the boathouse, next to the corner of the building. It was just out of sight of the boat. There, tacked up to the weathered wood siding, was a note and a banana peel.

"Ha!" laughed Peter, thinking Henrik was playing some kind of dumb joke. "I'll bet Uncle Morten ate your banana, after all. And look, there's even a little thank-you note."

"That's not a thank-you note," said Henrik, grabbing the small scrap of paper. He let the banana peel fall to the ground.

"So what's it say?" asked Peter.

"It's note number three."

Peter studied the scribbled message. Henrik was right. It was even written on the same kind of paper as the other two notes.

And in the same childish handwriting, he made out the words: *I haven't forgotten you. There's more to come.*

While Henrik looked around the boathouse to see if there were any other notes, Peter stared at the note and sighed. It was no joke, after all—and now Peter felt as though he was getting a headache. "More to come," he said quietly to himself. "I thought we already had seen it all."

9

BEACHED WHALE

"It can only mean one thing," pronounced Elise the next morning. Everyone in the family had come down to the boatyard early to see the *Anna Marie* pulled out of the water on a giant cart.

"What's that?" asked Peter. He stood off to the side with Elise, watching the man at the controls of the chugging gas motor that pulled the cable attached to the cart. Henrik was on the other side of the boat helping Uncle Morten and Grandfather Andersen rig up the high-pressure sprayer they would use to clean the bottom.

"The note," Elise yelled as the cart rolled slowly up a small railway to the boatyard. The fishing boat was rising out of the harbor a foot at a time, like a giant blue beached whale.

Peter stared at the boat emerging from the harbor's green water. Below the waterline, the boat had been painted a copper red to prevent the growth of seaweed. But it had been more than a year since the boat had been painted, and there was a jungle crop of sea lettuce, volcano-shaped barnacles, and thick slime.

"Peter, did you hear me?" Elise looked at her brother, but Peter was daydreaming again. "I think I know what the note means."

The boat lurched for a moment, and the man at the controls,

Mr. Madsen, muttered something rude under his breath. Elise raised her eyebrows but said nothing.

"Okay, so what does it mean?" asked Peter. "Uncle Morten doesn't know, so how can you possibly know what it means when he doesn't?"

Elise pulled him aside, away from the chugging of the little work engine. "Because Uncle Morten has other things to think about," she told him. "But it's simple."

"'More to come,'" Peter repeated the words of the note. "More what? More fire?"

Elise nodded. "Obviously. But I think whoever set the fire on the *Anna Marie* is going to try it again soon. Maybe tonight."

"But don't you think Uncle Morten would have thought of that? He said the notes aren't even worth calling the police over. They're just some kid's prank."

"Well, Uncle Morten has had his head in the clouds lately," she admitted.

Peter shook his head. "I know, Elise, but what can we do about it? Keld Poulsen hasn't been at school all week. You think it's somebody else, but we don't have any other suspects. And I'm not going back into Keld's place to sneak around."

"We'll just have to find out some other way."

"Well, the only other way I can think of"—Peter wrinkled his face the way he did when he was working out a problem—"is to catch whoever is doing it red-handed. And if you really think it's going to happen tonight, maybe we should guard the boat."

"Peter, I'm trying to be serious. Mom and Dad would never let us do that."

"Well, I'm trying to be serious, too." Peter looked around. The *Anna Marie*, dripping with its full crop of seaweed, was at the top of the boatyard railway. A small pit under the boat would allow them a place to work on the bottom of the craft. Satisfied, Mr. Madsen shut off the sputtering work engine.

"Hey, you two," Henrik yelled a minute later. "Your uncle says we can work the sprayer."

"Me first!" shouted the twins at the same time.

Holding the spray nozzle was the fun part. It almost wasn't work, Peter thought. While one of them watched the electric pump and the other kept the long hose untangled, the third stood beside the big fishing boat or climbed into the pit underneath to blast the sides with a concentrated stream of water.

"Hey, watch it!" yelled Peter. He came out of a fog of spray with a green blob of seaweed splattered on his forehead. Elise, who was watching the pump, burst out laughing. Peter only sputtered and wiped his face.

"I'm not going to untangle this hose if you keep spraying slime at me," he threatened Henrik.

"Sorry, old pal." Henrik grinned. "First time I've tried this, you know."

But when it was Peter's turn to spray, he made sure Henrik was soaked to the skin, too. All three of them were dripping by the time they had the hull mostly clean.

They chased each other with handfuls of seaweed until Uncle Morten discovered them.

"Hey!" he shouted from the deck. "Are you done down there?"

"We've done as much as we can with the water, Uncle Morten," answered Elise.

"That's good work," he said after he had climbed down to inspect the hull. "I owe each of you a bonus."

Henrik gave a pile of rubbish one last shot with the high-pressure hose, sending several cans clattering across the concrete.

"Henrik!" Peter put up his hand. "Do that again."

"What, spray a bunch of trash?"

"No." Peter gathered several cans into a pile. "I think I have an idea. Spray these cans."

Henrik obliged and hit the cans with a stream of water. The cans went clattering as before.

"That's it!" cried Peter. "I know what we can do. We can set an alarm!"

He ran over to the pile of cans, fished out two, and hit them together.

"String," he told the others. "All I need is some string."

By lunchtime Peter's contraption was nearly ready. It wasn't hard to find empty cans—dumpsters around the boatyard were full of them.

"Yech," complained Elise. "Are you sure you want all these? This one smells as though it's been in the dumpster for months."

"We'll need just a couple more," said Peter. "We can rinse them out if we need to."

Elise held her nose and rinsed one under a faucet, while Henrik finished poking holes in the cans with a hammer and a long nail. Peter threaded them all together.

"There," he announced. "What do you think? Are thirty-five cans enough?"

"Depends on how big the crook is," said Henrik. "Seems like plenty to me."

"Are you sure this is going to work, Peter?" asked Elise.

"Of course," Peter answered. "All we need to do is put some weight in the first can. Then we pile them all on the deck above, set the tripline, and—"

"And the person who trips over the string down here gets it all on his head," finished Henrik. "Then hopefully the security guard will hear the racket and come running."

A slow smile crept over Elise's face. "Pure genius."

"Well, for once *I* came up with an idea," said Peter. "Now all we have to do is test it."

"Let's wait until all the grown-ups are gone," suggested Henrik, scanning the boatyard. By that time, Peter's mother was coming with a plateful of food and a large pitcher of ice water for the workers.

"What's this?" asked Uncle Morten from up above on the boat. "Looks as if someone's going to have a picnic right here in the boatyard."

"I can't think of a better place!" declared Grandfather Andersen. Peter's mother produced a large blue tablecloth, while Peter and Henrik set up boards across two sawhorses.

"Is this the picnic?" Everyone turned to see Lisbeth von Schreider, her arms loaded with a picnic basket. She stood shyly at the edge of the work area.

"Lisbeth!" Uncle Morten slid down the ladder like a fireman when he saw her.

"Not so close!" she warned. "You're a mess."

"What?" Uncle Morten dusted his pants off, shook the sawdust from his hair, and grinned. "I thought you weren't going to return from Copenhagen until tonight."

"I couldn't wait to see how the boat was coming along," she replied with a smile. "My folks are doing fine."

Everyone cleaned up under the faucet by the little shed that housed the hoist controls while Peter's mother and Lisbeth set up the food.

It is a great spot for a picnic, Peter thought as he listened to all the excited chatter. And the picnic was almost the way they used to be before the war. There were open-faced rye bread sandwiches with sliced eggs, liver paste sandwiches, sliced cucumber salad, and, of course, pickled herring sandwiches.

"I forgot to bring knives and forks," said Mrs. Andersen, "so you're going to have to eat these with your fingers. I apologize."

Even though it wasn't usual for Danes to eat these kinds of treats without silverware, no one seemed to mind.

"Where did you get all this food?" asked Uncle Morten. "I haven't had a good liver paste sandwich in five years."

Peter's mother just grinned and smiled at Lisbeth. "I have my suppliers," she said. "We had a special shipment from Sweden. Lisbeth brought it."

Peter glanced over at Henrik, who was staring across the harbor in the direction of Sweden with a worried expression. But before Peter could say anything, Henrik snapped his head back and looked down at his food.

After Grandfather had prayed for the meal, and after everyone had oohed and ahhed about the food for several minutes, they got down to serious eating. Everyone found boxes to sit on around the homemade table, and no one seemed to mind the work going on around them in the boatyard.

While Peter listened, the adults chatted about the boat, about people they knew, and about the health of Lisbeth's parents. Henrik added a few comments about the latest soccer scores.

Peter took another slice of bread with pickled herring, closed his eyes, and took a deep breath. There was no mistaking the wonderful patchwork of boatyard smells—the water, the paint, even the thick, spicy aroma of the seaweed soup they had blasted off the bottom of the fishing boat. When he mixed in the clean, salty aroma of the herring sandwich, Peter could almost imagine he was far out at sea. Only he couldn't feel any waves.

Halfway through the cheeses, Uncle Morten picked up a nail and tapped it against his bottle of orange soda—the way people announce a toast.

"I'd like to make a toast"—his big voice seemed to vibrate above the hammering in the boatyard—"a toast to the safe return of the Melchior family."

They raised their sodas and tapped them against the bottle of the person sitting beside them.

"*Skoal!*" everyone cried, repeating the traditional toast. "Cheers!"

Peter looked over at Henrik, who was wiping his eyes with a handkerchief. For a moment he tried to imagine what it would be like without his parents, having to live with someone else's family. It would be hard, he decided, even staying with a good friend.

While everyone took a sip of the Swedish sodas Lisbeth had supplied, Uncle Morten cleared his throat once more.

"And another toast," he announced.

"Absolutely!" agreed Grandfather Andersen, not hesitating to raise his glass.

"Well, wait a minute, Dad. You don't know what you're toasting."

Grandfather Andersen, in a playful mood, bowed to his son. "Proceed. I'm terribly sorry."

"Yes, well, don't be too sorry. I have a very special toast—and a very special announcement."

Peter caught a glance of Lisbeth hiding behind her soda. Her cheeks were flushed. He was sure he knew what his uncle was going to say.

Uncle Morten took a deep breath and cleared his throat. "I'd like to make a toast to Miss Lisbeth von Schreider, who has agreed to change her name to Lisbeth Andersen!"

Uncle Morten stood up with his glass in the air, pulling Lisbeth with him. Everyone in the group stared up with big eyes at the couple, and no one said a word. In the distance someone's power tool whined, and a hammer pounded. Then Peter's mother exploded with a muffled shriek. "Oh, Morten!" Elise started giggling, and they surrounded Uncle Morten and Lisbeth in a group hug.

"We'll be married two weeks from today," put in Lisbeth. "I know it may seem like short notice, but I told Morten I would marry him as soon as he finished repairing this old boat."

"I knew it! I knew it!" repeated Grandfather Andersen as he pumped his son's hand and gave Lisbeth a big kiss on the cheek. "Morten couldn't have picked a better girl. That's why it's taken him so many years to choose."

Peter's father pounded his brother on the back, adding his congratulations.

"You've finally done it, you rascal!" said Mr. Andersen, grinning wider than Peter had ever seen. Peter and Henrik waited their turn as Elise jumped up and down in excitement.

"Two weeks!" she exclaimed.

"May 26," added Lisbeth.

As Peter took his uncle's big hand, he glanced over at his sister. For an instant, his blood ran cold.

"Elise," he called. "Watch where you're stepping!"

But it was too late. Not thinking, Elise had backed up behind the table, and her foot had caught on the kite string they had attached to the can alarm before lunch. She tripped, pulling the string with her.

Peter looked up at the back end of the boat, just above their heads. The trap was working too well. He had just enough time to duck before the first part came tumbling down in a clattering racket.

"Everyone duck!" Peter shouted as the string of cans fell on top of them.

The trap hit Uncle Morten first, but he put up his arm so it tangled around him without hitting Lisbeth.

"Ow!" said Henrik, ducking. "That one hit me on the head."

They looked around at the mess of cans and string that had snaked its way around everyone standing or sitting near the boat. Uncle Morten was caught, as were Lisbeth, Peter, Henrik, and Elise.

"Ooh, I'm sorry," Elise apologized as she tried to step away from the mess. "Is everyone all right?"

"We're fine," answered Lisbeth. She fanned her hands out through the tangle of string. "But what is all this?"

"It was my idea," confessed Peter. "It's supposed to be a burglar alarm."

"Looks like the wedding bells rang a little early," joked Peter's father, and he started laughing.

Pretty soon everyone joined in the laughter. Mr. Andersen waded through the mess of cans and string to give Uncle Morten and Lisbeth another hug.

"Congratulations, you two," he said. Then he looked at Peter. "And I think if there's anyone to catch, Peter and the gang will be sure to do it."

If there's anyone to catch, thought Peter, untangling himself, *I hope we get him.* At least he knew the burglar alarm worked.

He looked over in the direction of their boathouse just in time to see someone walking quickly away from the corner. Peter blinked, but he was sure he had looked straight into the face of Keld Poulsen.

10

Up From the Ashes

"Well, one thing's for sure," declared Henrik as he tipped back on a crate in the boathouse later that Saturday afternoon. "Your uncle isn't thinking about anything except getting married right now. No offense, but—"

"Yeah, I know." Peter shook his head. "Now we know why he's been so dreamy lately. And why he hasn't paid much attention to the notes."

Elise leaned against the chicken wire of the pigeon coop and looked at their birds. "Well, what's wrong with that? You'd be that way, too, if you were getting married."

Peter just whooped. "Oh really?"

"I take that back," said Elise. "You're probably going to be thinking about boats, or birds, or working on your stamp collection right up until the day you get married."

"Hey, I know what's important," answered Peter. He ran his fingers through his blond hair, twisting a piece of it around his finger. "In fact, speaking of birds, when are we going to do some flying? Henrik?"

Peter and Elise looked over to where Henrik was kneeling on

the floor in front of the birds. He was holding a dried pea between his teeth, waiting for one of the birds to take it from his mouth.

"Henrik, what are you doing?" asked Elise.

"Washilooklike?" mumbled Henrik without opening his mouth. "Henrik Melchior, mashter animal trainer."

One of the birds had caught sight of the pea and was investigating. "Henrik, are you really going to feed the bird like that?" Peter asked.

"Uh-huh. Shh."

"That's disgusting," Elise said. "I can't believe you'd want to do that."

Peter wrinkled his nose as the bird stepped closer to the chicken-wire divider. Henrik poked his mouth through the wire, and finally the bird reached over and pecked the pea from Henrik's teeth.

"Taste good?" asked Peter.

Henrik grinned. "You try it."

"No way," replied Elise, wiping her mouth. "You can probably catch all kinds of diseases from those birds."

"Yeah, like lockjaw!" Henrik gripped his face and fell over on the floor as Peter fished another dried pea from the bag of pigeon food up on a shelf.

"Peter, don't you dare," warned Elise.

"Don't worry, I'm not going to feed it to the birds," replied Peter as he popped the animal food into his mouth. "I just want to see why they like this stuff so much."

Henrik and Elise stared at Peter as he chewed on the dried pea. It tasted like a cross between a piece of dirt and a wad of stale cardboard. But Peter kept chewing and smiling.

"This is great, Elise," he told his sister, looking for somewhere he could spit it out. "I can see why the pigeons like it."

"Really?" Elise raised her eyebrow suspiciously. "You look pale."

Peter started to choke, and the other two laughed at his act.

"Here, spit it out in the trash," Elise told him, giggling. Peter did, but he couldn't get the stale taste out of his mouth.

"That *looked* delicious, Peter," laughed Henrik. "I told you it tasted great."

"Yeah, it did," agreed Peter, laughing at himself. "But what about the flying we were going to do?"

Henrik sat up, undid the latch to the door of the pigeon coop, and stepped inside. "How about right now?"

It took Henrik a minute to trap the birds while Peter looked for the basket they used to carry their homing pigeons.

"Where is the basket, Elise?" he asked, looking under Grandfather Andersen's workbench.

"I don't know," she answered. "We haven't used it in so long."

"I know where it is," said Henrik. The twins stopped their search. "I left it back in Sweden."

"Oh, yeah." Peter stood and dusted his knees. "You used it to carry your bird."

"Well, it doesn't matter," concluded Elise, holding up a small wooden box. "We can use this if we just cover the top with a rag and tie it down."

"Great!" Peter readied the box while the other two caught the pigeons. Then Peter held the top open as Henrik carefully placed the squirming birds inside. It took several tries, but finally they had all the birds in the box and an old towel draped over the top.

"That's all three," said Peter, checking the knot he had tied to hold the towel. "So where do we go?"

Elise picked up the basket. "Let's not go far. Maybe just to the other side of the railroad station. We need to let them get used to flying again."

"Yeah, I hope they haven't forgotten the way home," laughed Henrik. They walked together to the other side of town, away from the Kronborg Castle and toward the railroad station.

Peter looked around the unfamiliar neighborhood. "Far enough?"

"Just a few more blocks," said Elise, taking a turn carrying the bird box. She glanced at the railroad tracks to their left and wrinkled her eyebrows. "You know, I have a bad feeling."

Peter looked at his sister. "What, about the birds?"

"No." Elise shook her head. "About Uncle Morten and Lisbeth."

"Oh, the lovebirds," giggled Henrik.

"Henrik!" scolded Elise. "I'm not trying to be funny. I have this terrible feeling something awful is going to happen before the wedding."

"You mean with the boat?" asked Henrik.

Elise nodded, and Henrik frowned.

"And since Keld saw the trap," added Peter, "he knows all about it."

"But look," said Elise. "We already decided that we need a better way to find out if Keld set the fire. I think we need to try to get a handwriting match."

"That would be better than a shoe match." Henrik looked both ways before they crossed another street. "Lots of people could have the same footprint, or the same size shoe. We should get Keld to write something for us."

"Right," laughed Peter. "While he's busy trying on the shoe we found."

"Maybe that's not such a strange idea," Henrik suggested. "Peter, maybe you could get into his desk during recess and borrow his language writing book. There would be enough writing there to compare to the note."

"Wait a minute." Peter crossed his arms and set his chin. "That sounds too much like the plan to sneak into his apartment and check his shoes. I'm not going—"

"Don't worry." Henrik looked around and lowered his voice in case anyone besides the pigeons was listening. "Although we are pretty close to his apartment right now."

Peter looked around at the neighborhood and realized Henrik was right. "Let's let the birds go," he said.

"What about over there?" Elise pointed at a small playground, really a courtyard between two tall buildings.

"All we need to do is keep an eye on Keld in school next Monday," continued Henrik. "Wait until he writes something and throws it away. Then we fetch it out of the wastebasket."

"That's assuming he shows up for class," said Peter. "I'll bet the reason he's been home sick is because of that awful cigar we saw him smoking."

"I'm sure glad he's not in my class," said Elise. She pulled the towel off the top of the box and held it up, but none of the birds moved.

"They forgot how to fly," said Peter, peeking into the box. "Come on, birds!"

One of the pigeons finally scrambled over the backs of the other two and jumped into the late afternoon air. The others followed a second later in a fluttering of wings.

"There they go," shouted Henrik. He craned his neck to follow the birds' flight.

But instead of circling the area and heading straight home—as they used to do—the birds headed for the nearest roof and quickly landed.

"Hey, what are they doing?" asked Peter. He ran over to the building, a two-story row-house apartment, and clapped his hands. The birds only hopped up on a dormer window.

"Those silly birds," muttered Henrik. "They've forgotten how to fly."

"No." Elise put her hand up to her forehead to shade the sun. "They just need a little help."

She looked around at the ground, then picked up a small handful of pebbles. "Here," she told the boys. "If we can just get them to fly, they'll be back home in no time."

The three of them tried to bounce the pebbles off the roof as close as they could to the birds without actually hitting them. Henrik got the closest, and one of the birds flapped its wings. Then a window flew open on one of the roof dormers.

"Hey!" yelled a husky man. "What do you think you're doing? If you don't stop throwing rocks, I'm going to come down there and . . ."

The kids didn't wait to hear the rest of the grizzled sailor-type's threat. All three ran down the street as fast as they could, away from the voice. They were only half a block away when Henrik stopped.

"The box," he puffed. "We forgot the box."

"Oh no," moaned Peter.

"I doesn't matter," said Elise. "Leave it there."

But Peter made a quick U-turn and returned to the spot where they had left the pigeon box. A quick glance up at the roof told him the pigeons were gone—and there was no sailor in sight.

"Got it," said Peter when he returned to where the others were waiting.

"I can't believe I threw pebbles like that," Elise was saying. "What a dumb idea."

"I thought it was a good idea," said Henrik, looking back at the apartment house. "The birds took off, didn't they?"

"Yeah." Peter handed his sister the box. She was still shaking her head.

"I still can't believe I did that," she repeated. "I've been hanging around you boys too much."

Henrik smiled. "Some people are just lucky."

Peter looked around. They had run into a part of town they normally stayed away from—Keld Poulsen's neighborhood.

"Since we're here, you know what we should do?" asked Henrik.

Peter shook his head. "Uh-uh, Henrik. I know what you're thinking."

"No, you don't," replied Henrik, looking up and down the street. "I was just thinking that since we're near Keld's place, maybe we should just, well, keep an eye on things. See if we can find him."

"And then what?" asked Peter. He remembered the last time

he had agreed to go to Keld's apartment. "What if he's inside, looking out his window?"

"We won't get close enough for him to see us," Henrik promised. "Maybe just follow him."

"Wonderful," replied Peter. He looked down a side street. "So what if we don't see him?" Peter still wasn't convinced it was a good idea to go anywhere near Keld's place.

"We'll just wait outside his place for a while," pronounced Henrik. "Maybe down by the railroad tracks, where we can see his front door, but he can't see us. What do you think, Elise?"

Elise looked from Henrik to Peter, then shook her head. "I don't think it's a good idea. You two can stay if you want. I'm going home to see if the birds got back." Without another word, she left.

"Fine." Henrik shrugged. "So it's just us, Peter."

"Yeah," whispered Peter. "I guess so." For a minute he thought of running after Elise, but instead he followed Henrik down the street in the opposite direction. Five minutes later they had positioned themselves beside a railroad car, half a block from Keld's front door.

"Which door is it?" whispered Peter.

"I don't think he can hear you," remarked Henrik in a louder voice from where he crouched beside a railroad track. "It's the place right above the pub, remember?"

Peter sat down with Henrik and stared at the old apartment house. He would rather have been down at the boathouse, walking around the harbor, fishing—anything but sitting there spying on Keld Poulsen's apartment. Five minutes went by, then ten.

"Seen anything yet?" said Elise from behind them.

Peter twirled around and smiled. "Elise! What are you doing here? You didn't already go home, did you?"

Elise half shrugged. "I checked on the birds, just to make sure they got back okay. But I couldn't leave you guys alone, could I? You'd get in trouble."

"Nobody's getting in trouble," said Henrik, not taking his eyes off Keld's door.

Peter winked at his sister. "Okay, Henrik, but we're never going to see Keld waiting like this."

"We just have to be more patient," replied Henrik.

Peter resigned himself to waiting. While some of Helsingor's more questionable-looking sailors and characters pushed their way into the pub, Peter counted sea gulls flying over the harbor.

"See anything yet?" he asked over his shoulder. Even Elise was getting fidgety.

"Not yet," replied Henrik.

"I think it's getting close to dinnertime," said Peter after another fifteen minutes of watching. "We need to get home."

"Just five more minutes, Peter," protested Henrik. "We've waited this long. Maybe he'll come out right after we leave."

"Okay, five minutes." But they didn't need that much time. Peter had hardly spoken the words when the door to Keld's apartment opened and someone stepped out.

"Hey, look!" Henrik hissed and grabbed Peter's arm. All three of them jumped a little farther behind the boxcar they were leaning against, then Peter peeked around to see.

"It's him!" Peter whispered urgently.

"Finally." Henrik gave them a thumbs-up sign. He tiptoed around to the other side of the boxcar and beckoned for the others to follow.

They followed a half block behind Keld, who seemed as if he were out for a stroll. An innocent Saturday evening walk. The boy turned left, and Henrik looked around the corner before motioning the others to continue.

"Where did he go?" whispered Peter, checking around the corner as well.

"Shh!" insisted Henrik. "I think he went into that store up the street."

"No, he didn't," replied Elise. "He's up by that bakery."

Just like in most other Danish cities, the stores were easy to spot. Shoemakers had the shape of a boot over their names. Butchers had signs shaped like the head of a cow. And the bakeries had pretzel-shaped signs hanging over the door.

The three held back for a moment, huddling together.

"If he comes out, he's going to see us for sure," warned Peter.

"Too late." Elise observed as Keld popped out from under the pretzel sign with a little cloth sack in his hand.

There was nowhere to go, no handy doorway where they could all hide. No farther away than Peter could throw a breakfast roll, Keld stood and stared straight at them.

"Act natural!" whispered Henrik, untangling himself from behind Peter. He pulled the other two alongside him, and they tumbled down the sidewalk toward the bakery.

Keld wiped the surprise from his face and started walking in their direction with big strides. While Henrik hugged the gutter, Keld wordlessly marched straight ahead.

As they passed one another going opposite directions, Peter caught a whiff of the bread in Keld's sack.

"We're pretty good spies, huh?" Peter whispered to his sister as soon as they were around the next corner. "Now we know where Keld buys bread for his mom."

Henrik playfully punched him on the shoulder. "We'll just have to try again," he insisted.

Peter had heard his friend say *that* before.

11

ANOTHER SUSPECT

Most mornings Peter got up early to read his little pocket Bible. That Sunday morning, though, he let himself sleep in a bit. After all, church wasn't until eleven.

But when Peter woke to the sound of pebbles hitting his window, he knew he wasn't going to be able to sleep. For a second, he smiled.

Henrik used to do this all the time, he thought, *before he had to go to Sweden.*

"You should have knocked," Peter called down to the street after he yanked his window open. But then he realized something wasn't quite right, and he shook his head. *What's Henrik doing down on the street?*

Peter glanced back at the cot in his room where Henrik had been sleeping. The covers were thrown back.

"Knocked? I couldn't do that," answered Henrik with one of his big grins. "Didn't want to wake you up."

Peter grinned back and shook his head. Then he thought of his parents who were probably trying to sleep in. He put his finger to his lips.

"Shh!" he warned. "My parents."

"Oh, right. Peter, I've got to tell you something. You won't believe who I just saw—and who was with him."

"What are you doing outside already? It's only seven." Peter wasn't sure what his friend was talking about.

"Couldn't sleep this morning, so I decided to go for a walk. I locked myself out by accident." Henrik was letting his voice get louder, and Peter put his finger to his lips again. By that time, Elise had tiptoed into Peter's room, and she waved at Henrik over Peter's shoulder.

"Oh, hi, Elise," continued Henrik. "I'll just tell you both."

Peter looked back at his sister and frowned. At least she was dressed, he thought.

"So who did you see?" asked Peter. By that time he was getting curious.

Henrik looked around the sidewalk, but there was no one else on the street—except a man out for a morning walk with his dog at the end of the block.

"Well, you two were still asleep," he began, "and I went out for a walk. I even walked by Keld's place again, just in case."

"So did you see him?" asked Elise, moving up beside Peter at the window.

"I saw him, all right." Henrik rubbed his hands together as he told his story. "I followed him all the way through the old part of town, and—"

"Did he see you?" asked Peter.

"Of course he didn't see me," answered Henrik. "I followed him downtown—"

"Wait, wait, wait," interrupted Peter. "I can't hear half of what you're saying. Elise and I are coming down."

"Well, I could talk louder," offered Henrik, but Peter had already turned to run down the stairs so he could let Henrik in.

"Okay, start over. You say you saw Keld."

"Right," confirmed Henrik as he climbed the stairs leading to the Andersens' living room. "It was really early this morning. He went down to the old part of town, past the Saint Olai Church. And then this man came up and grabbed him."

"Grabbed him?" asked Elise. "Where were you?"

"Who grabbed him?" Peter asked as he sat down at the top of the stairs. "Did you see?"

Henrik held up his hands. "Yeah, I saw the man, but I was hiding behind the corner of a building. I don't know who he was. I've never seen him before."

"So what did he do?" questioned Peter.

"Well, he grabbed Keld like this—" Henrik squeezed Peter's shoulder with one hand.

"Ow!" cried Peter. "I get what you mean."

"Sorry, you wanted to know," Henrik apologized before continuing his story. "Well, this man locked on to Keld's shoulder and wouldn't let. It looked like Keld was scared, but they stood there talking for about ten minutes. No, maybe five. Anyway, it seemed like a long time. I could tell Keld wasn't having much fun.

"So here was Keld," he continued in a dramatic tone, "practically on his knees, begging this man to let him go, or something, I don't know. And then this rough-looking teenager walked up, and they were all talking."

"You didn't hear what they said?" asked Elise.

"No. But I'm getting to that. At first I couldn't hear what was going on, but then they turned around, and I thought Keld was going to see me. All three of them were walking in my direction with Keld following behind them like a puppy dog. I had to duck behind a garbage can."

Peter couldn't believe it. "What if they saw you?"

"I told you they didn't. But when they were walking by, I caught part of what they were saying."

"And?" Elise nearly fell down the stairs as she leaned closer to hear Henrik's story.

"Keld was saying, 'Okay, Friday night, two weeks from today. Nine o'clock. I'll help you get it all ready. Just let me go.' Keld seemed to be begging the man. And then the man said, 'Go home, Keld. Come on, Frits. You'll help me with the boat. And not a word of this to Madsen.' "

"You're sure they said Friday night in two weeks?" asked Peter, waving his hands in excitement. "The night before Uncle Morten is getting married?"

Elise stood up and started pacing. "That's the night before the wedding, all right. The man really said 'You'll help me with the boat'? Did he mention anything else about the boat, or about setting it on fire?"

Henrik shook his head. "Uh-uh. Just what I told you. 'Friday night. Nine o'clock.' That's all I heard."

"And that's all you saw?" asked Peter.

"Pretty much," answered Henrik. "The man looked tough."

"Hmm," murmured Elise. Then she turned to Henrik. "Too bad you didn't have a camera with you to take a picture of those other two people. We could have used a photo."

Peter ran into the kitchen, yanked open a drawer, and pulled out a stack of lined binder paper. He threw it down on the kitchen table with a pencil and pointed to Elise.

"So what if we don't have a picture," he declared. "All we have to do is make one ourselves."

Henrik didn't get it. "What do you mean? Just draw a picture?"

"No, not just draw a picture," replied Peter. "I mean make a sketch, like the police do when they're looking for a suspect. And we have our artist right here."

Henrik picked up the pencil. "Oh, okay. All I have to do is tell Elise what the mystery man looks like, and she can draw him for us."

"Well, I don't know," objected Elise. "I've never—"

"But you've done lots of faces, Elise," argued Peter. "I've seen you do them. Look, I'll even go get some books with photos of people's faces in them so Henrik can get a better idea. And why don't you let Henrik look at your sketchbook?"

"There's nothing good in there," she replied.

"Oh, come on," insisted Peter. "There are some great pictures."

Peter ran over to the living-room bookshelf and pulled out several volumes. The *Who, What, Where* yearbook of news events and people. A book of politics. A history book. He vaulted over Tiger on his way back to the kitchen.

"Watch out, kitty. You shouldn't be out walking just yet." He gently placed his cat in the kitchen basket, then returned to the table.

"Look," he said, "these books show lots of different faces. Start with the teenager Frits."

Henrik started leafing through the books and pointing out different features. Elise studied them carefully, then began her sketch.

"This shape head?" she asked, pointing to a picture of the king.

"Kind of," replied Henrik. "He has the king's nose, anyway. And these ears—wait, no, these." He laughed when he saw Elise pencil in the details.

"Hair down to there," he instructed her. "Kind of dirty looking, like he hadn't taken a bath in a long time."

A half hour later, he stood back and studied the sketch.

"Almost there." He closed his eyes, then peeked again at the drawing. "Yeah, that's Frits, all right. I can't believe how good you are at this."

Elise blushed and fiddled with her eraser. "It's not that hard."

Henrik leafed through the rest of Elise's sketchbook, stopping to look at the pictures she had done while the twins had been in a German prison. Those pages were folded and wrinkled, stuffed in between other pages.

"This is really neat, Elise," he commented. He pulled out one more page and stared.

"Wow!" he cried, pointing to a drawing Elise had done months earlier. "That's him! I can't believe this. It looks exactly like the older man who was with Keld. Where did you get this?"

Peter yanked the book out of Henrik's hand and looked at the drawing. A glance told him who it was.

"Elise, do you know who this is?" Henrik asked.

Elise nodded seriously. "Of course I know. I drew it when we were in the German prison."

Peter tossed the notebook back into Henrik's lap. "It's Keld's dad."

12

ONE MORE PUZZLE

The hours seemed to drag as Peter looked up at the classroom clock one more time.

"Did you tell your sister to meet us in front of the cathedral right after school?" whispered Henrik. "This is the first day nobody needs us for errands in a week."

Henrik was right. Between wedding errands for Mrs. Andersen and boat errands for Uncle Morten, they hardly had time to do all the school assignments Mrs. Bernsted had been giving the class. Maybe it was the end of the year panic, but Peter thought his teacher had been loading them up with work as they tried to finish their math books.

It had been over a week since Elise had sketched the picture of the teenager Henrik had seen with Keld and his father.

"Shh," Peter whispered. Mrs. Bernsted stopped writing their homework assignments for a moment, then continued.

"I hope no one is whispering," Mrs. Bernsted warned them in her no-nonsense tone, "unless that person would like to stay after school. Remember, this is only Monday. There is a long week ahead."

Peter copied the homework assignment down as fast as he could without glancing over at Henrik. He hadn't been in trouble in school for a long time, and he didn't want to start now.

One row over and two seats ahead, Keld Poulsen crumpled up his paper in disgust and sent it sailing into the wastebasket. Peter saw Henrik look over at him, wink, and give a thumbs-up signal. This was what they had been waiting for! Peter looked around nervously.

While Mrs. Bernsted finished writing the assignment on the board in her careful script, Henrik carefully wadded a piece of paper from his binder and stood up as if to stretch. He slid over to the wastebasket, dropped his paper in, and then bent down to tie his shoelace. Out of the corner of his eye, Peter saw Henrik's hand slip into the wastebasket and fish around on the top for Keld's paper.

"Henrik, would you please take your seat?" commanded Mrs. Bernsted as she turned on the heels of her flat shoes. Henrik pulled back his hand in a flash and slinked back to his desk, while the teacher paced over to her big oak desk.

"Who is in charge of cleaning chalkboards today?"

In the front row, Ruth Glensvig raised her hand.

"Collecting the textbooks?" Two more hands went up. "Emptying the trash?"

Peter looked around. Annelise Kastrup, one row back, shot up her hand and smiled at the teacher.

Their teacher smiled back briefly, almost without looking up. "Thank you. You have three minutes until you're dismissed. While you four finish classroom chores, would the rest of you please straighten your desks and finish copying down your homework assignment?"

Mrs. Bernsted sure knew how to keep the class busy. Peter couldn't remember a time when anyone in the class wasn't doing something.

Peter glanced to his left, and Henrik gave him a disgusted look and held out an orange peel with some pencil shavings.

"I couldn't find it," he whispered.

Peter looked behind him to where Annelise was straightening out her desk. It was always perfect, so he wasn't sure what she was straightening out. But as she started to get up for the garbage, Peter stood up, too.

"I-I'll get it, Annelise," he offered. He had to. Peter and Henrik had been watching Keld the whole week, and Keld had never thrown anything out. This might be their only chance to find out if Keld's handwriting matched that on the mystery notes.

"What did you say?" Annelise gave Peter a confused look as she stood up.

"He said, 'I'll get it, darling Annelise,'" came a voice from behind Peter. Three or four kids nearby snickered.

Peter didn't look around, but he knew it was Jesper Jarl, Keld's old buddy. Peter's face instantly turned beet red, but for once he didn't care. While Annelise made gasping noises, Peter vaulted over his desk, grabbed the trash can, and disappeared out the door.

Everyone knows I'm not sweet on Annelise, Peter fumed as he stomped down the hallway to the janitor's closet. *I hope this was worth it.*

After some digging, Peter found Keld's crumpled note and stuffed it into his pocket. But he waited until the bell had rung and everyone was gone before he returned to the classroom.

"Hey, that was a great move." Henrik congratulated him outside the school. "But I didn't know about you and Annelise."

"Don't be silly," sniffed Peter as he fished the note out of his pocket. "At least I got this."

"So let's see. Is it the same handwriting?"

Henrik crowded in close to see what the note would tell them as Peter unfolded it.

"Aw, it's nothing," said Henrik, disappointed. "It's just a lot of doodles. No writing at all."

Henrik was right. Peter straightened out the wrinkled paper, but there was no actual handwriting there to compare to the other two notes. There were swirls, boxes, and something that looked like a cigar with wings, but no handwriting. And to think Peter had risked his reputation for doodles!

"Well, so much for this," Peter crumpled up the note and stuffed it into Henrik's shirt pocket. "What's your plan?"

Henrik brightened. "Come on. Elise will be waiting."

Elise was hopscotching up and down the front steps of the giant Helsingor cathedral when they trotted up. She craned her head back to look up at the tall, copper-roofed bell tower—the tallest point in Helsingor.

"What took you guys so long?"

"Peter had to help his girlfriend with her chores," teased Henrik.

"Henrik!" Peter grabbed Henrik's ear and started pulling.

"Ow!" Henrik bent over sideways. "Just kidding."

"Take it back," demanded Peter. Henrik looked over to make sure Peter was smiling.

"All right, I take it back." Henrik surrendered, and Peter let go. "But Annelise sure liked what you did for her. She was really smiling."

"She was not."

"Well, if she wasn't, she should have been."

Peter just frowned and held out the useless note to his sister. "We thought we had a sample of Keld's handwriting. He never throws anything away in class."

"You're kidding, right?" Elise looked at the doodles. "You're in the same class with this guy, and you don't even know what his handwriting looks like?"

Henrik just shrugged. "We never paid any attention to it before. Now that we've been looking for a sample for the past week we can't get it. He's been absent a lot."

Elise shook her head. "So what do we do now?"

Henrik started down the steps of the cathedral. "Do you have the drawing, Elise?"

She patted her schoolbag and nodded while Henrik explained

his plan. Helsingor High School was only a few blocks away on Mill Avenue.

————

"You want to identify the boy in a drawing?" The high-school secretary looked over her glasses and down her nose at the three kids. She took the sketch and studied it carefully. Peter scanned the office nervously.

What if she knows who it is, and the guy discovers someone was asking questions about him? Peter worried. *Or worse yet, what if he comes walking down the hallway right now and sees us through the glass door?*

Peter had never been inside the high school, and even though all the older kids were gone for the day, he felt as if he should be outside.

The woman shook her head. "I don't think so, but it's a very nice drawing. It almost looks professional. What did you say this was for?"

Henrik hesitated, but Peter could tell he had thought this through.

"My friend here drew it," Henrik explained with a nod toward Elise. "She's an artist, and we just wanted to find out the person's name to see if it was someone from around here. We know his name might be Frits, or something like that."

Elise looked embarrassed by the attention.

"I'm sorry, but I don't recognize the face. Or the name. Of course, I've only been here two years. A teacher might be able to tell you, but I think they're all gone for the day."

"I guess we'll have to come back," replied Henrik, slumping his shoulders.

Peter took another look at the office with its class pictures on the walls. He put his hand on Henrik's shoulder.

"Are those pictures from the past few years?" he asked, pointing at a series of photos stretching several feet. "Maybe we could look through them. . . ."

But after the fifteenth picture, the faces started to look the same. It was a large school with hundreds of students. In many of the photos, students had hidden behind people in front of them just as the photo was snapped.

Peter tried to see if the eyes peering from behind another student's head matched the drawing Elise had made. He wished he had a magnifying glass. And after studying a few half-blurry photos of tiny faces, he wasn't sure he would recognize their man if he were smiling from the front row.

"Look over here," called Elise. "I think this may be it." Peter didn't even glance up; at least a dozen faces had already looked like the right one. Henrik had given a thumbs-down to every one so far.

Henrik looked closely. "That's it! Yeah, that's him—well, maybe. It's so little. What's the name?"

A teacher walked through the office behind them just as Elise scanned the list at the bottom of the photo.

"Is there some way I can help you kids?" the teacher asked pleasantly. He almost looked like a high schooler himself, except that he carried a worn leather briefcase and wore a neatly trimmed gray moustache.

The secretary looked up from her typing. "Oh, Mr. Nygaard, I thought you were already gone. These young detectives are looking for a name. I don't recognize the face, but maybe you will."

The teacher looked over Elise's shoulder as she pointed to the tiny face on the photo. He compared the photo to Elise's picture and frowned.

"It's a very good drawing of Verner Norsk," he told them, pointing to the face Henrik had discovered. "That boy, right there."

The teacher got up to leave the office, but stopped with his hand on the doorknob. "You know about Verner?"

Peter wasn't sure he wanted to, now that he was staring at the frowning photo of a very mean-looking teenager.

"I'm not sure you want to know this boy," continued the teacher. "He didn't finish school, had to be removed from class. A real shame. He was a smart student. But I would stay away from him, if I were you. I've heard he's . . . well, you don't look like the type of kids to get involved with Verner Norsk."

Elise was still puzzled. "His name isn't Frits?"

"Frits . . . right." The teacher sounded as if he were remembering a bad dream. "That's what everyone called him. His real name is Verner, though. That was my first year of teaching. Almost my last. By now he's probably in—no, I shouldn't say that."

"Why was he kicked out of school?" pressed Henrik.

The teacher frowned once more. "There was the smoking in the bathrooms, the broken chairs, the fire in a wastebasket. . . you want to hear more? Those were the minor things, before all the Nazi stuff."

But that was enough for Peter. "I think that's all we need to know," he nodded at the teacher. "Right, Henrik?"

Even Henrik looked a little shaken. Verner "Frits" Norsk was certainly no choirboy.

"Umm, excuse me," said Henrik, "but what did you mean by 'Nazi stuff'?"

The teacher looked as if he had changed his mind about talking with them. "That's all over with now. This Verner character is probably long gone by now. Now, if you'll excuse me, please."

The young teacher was gone almost before they had a chance to thank him. They turned to leave, walking as fast as they dared down the polished tile of the main hallway. Outside, they raced each other to the boathouse.

"It worked," exclaimed Peter, holding up Elise's drawing once more. "Your drawing worked, Elise."

"Well, at least we have a name now." Elise took her drawing and studied it. "And now we have three suspects. Keld, Keld's dad, and this Frits fellow—or Verner, whatever his name is."

"Maybe they made Keld set the fire," guessed Peter. "And

they're going to finish off the job Friday."

"For once, Peter, it all sounds as though it's fitting together."
Henrik hit the workbench with his fist. "We better tell your uncle
everything—whether he wants to know or not."

13

SOUNDING THE ALARM

"But, Uncle Morten!" Peter's voice was desperate as he tried to convince his uncle. "You've got to believe us!"

"Yeah," added Henrik. "We would have told you about this sooner, but you've been in Copenhagen for the past three days."

Uncle Morten threw up his hands. "I'm sorry, kids, but I'm not sure I understand what you're saying. Now, tell me again. What did you see? And who?"

Peter began again. "Henrik saw Keld with his father and someone named Verner Norsk, and he overheard them planning to do something to the boat Friday night. That's tonight!"

"What exactly did they say was going to happen tonight?" asked Uncle Morten, blowing the sawdust from the doorframe of the *Anna Marie*. The boat was still up on the blocks, but it was looking more and more like it used to.

Peter dug his toe into the dirt. "Well, he didn't give any details, did he Henrik?"

Henrik shook his head.

"But, Uncle Morten," continued Peter, "with all the notes, the shoe, Keld hanging around the pier watching us, and now this

Verner Norsk, aren't you just a little worried? It all adds up."

Uncle Morten stopped sanding long enough to look straight at Peter, Elise, and Henrik. "Look, I appreciate everything you've done, but we really don't have anything concrete. But just to be safe, I'll have Mr. Madsen keep an eye on the boatyard tonight. Does that make you feel better?"

"But, Uncle Morten," protested Peter. "What if Mr. Madsen doesn't catch whoever is doing this and something happens to the *Anna Marie*? That boat is your life!"

Uncle Morten shook his head. "Not my life, Peter. Just the way I make my living. Don't forget, I'm getting married tomorrow. I've got more on my mind than playing detective."

"I'll say," Henrik mumbled under his breath. He wasn't going to give up so easily. "But what about Keld's dad? Aren't the police after him?"

Uncle Morten nodded and went back to his work. "I almost wish you kids would have told me that sooner. The police *are* after him. If that really was him that you saw, I can't believe he plans to stay here in the city where people would recognize him. He's going to try to escape Denmark any time now."

"It was him," insisted Henrik. "I know it was."

"Well, it's certainly possible," agreed Uncle Morten, "but there are a lot of men who look like him. It could have been anyone."

"What about Frits?" asked Peter.

Uncle Morten just shook his head and put up his hands in surrender. "I've never heard that name or seen that face before. He doesn't know me. Why would he set the *Anna Marie* on fire?"

"Well, he knows Mr. Poulsen, and he has plenty of reasons," countered Elise.

"Not really. Sure, he knows who I am and what I was doing in the Underground. But I don't think he would destroy my boat."

"But don't you know anyone who might want revenge?" asked Peter.

Uncle Morten just blew out his breath. "I don't think so, kids. The war is over."

"But—" Henrik was getting frustrated when a knock on the hull of the boat distracted the little group.

"Yoo-hoo," came Lisbeth's voice. "Is anyone up there?"

Uncle Morten's face lit up, and the boat shook as he scampered to the railing to look down. "Right here!"

"Honestly, Morten, we're getting married tomorrow, and you're busy working on this boat of yours!"

"But you told me that you wouldn't marry me until the boat was finished, right?" replied Uncle Morten, checking his watch. "And that leaves me only twenty-six hours and seven minutes to finish the job."

"Well, I think you're close enough to being finished for now. We have a wedding rehearsal dinner to go to in"—she checked her own wristwatch and smiled back at him—"in sixty-seven minutes and twenty seconds."

Henrik and Peter gave each other a confused look as Uncle Morten made for the ladder.

"Isn't the wedding tomorrow?" asked Henrik.

"Of course," Lisbeth replied. "We just wanted to have a nice evening with all the people who are going to be in the wedding. You're invited to the dinner, too. And Elise. She's going to be our flower girl."

Uncle Morten winked at the boys. "I have to go clean up," he told them.

"Flower girl?" asked Henrik, confused. "What's that?"

Elise looked over her shoulder at the boys with a small grin. "A flower girl is like a bridesmaid, only she carries flowers for the bride and groom. It's an American custom."

Peter looked to his uncle to explain.

"I had never heard of it, either." Uncle Morten shrugged. "But Lisbeth read in a magazine that Americans have flower girls in their weddings and thought it would be fun to have one. And a first man and honor maiden, too."

"That's best man and maid of honor," corrected Lisbeth. "And we need to go, Morten."

Uncle Morten winked at the boys as he left. "Dinner will be after the short rehearsal," he told them. "Don't forget to be at the parsonage by six."

"Sure, Uncle Morten," replied Peter.

Henrik just shook his head as Uncle Morten and Elise disappeared over the side. "Flower girl! Huh."

They watched Elise leave with Uncle Morten and Lisbeth, and Henrik frowned.

"Why doesn't your uncle believe us?"

"He believes us," replied Peter, coming to his uncle's defense. "He just has a lot on his mind."

"Well, he's going to have a lot more on his mind if Frits manages to burn up the boat. It's just sitting here out in the open."

Peter looked around at the deck of the *Anna Marie*. The new deckhouse was done; only a few unpainted pieces of trim remained around the roof. *We can't let them burn up the* Anna Marie, *not after all our work,* he thought.

"They sure fixed it up in a hurry, huh?" Henrik sat down on the edge of the boat and opened and closed the new door.

"Yeah, I guess. Hey, Henrik, whatever happened to our can alarm?"

They searched the deck of the boat until they found a tangled pile of cans and string.

Henrik picked up one of the cans and tried to unravel the mess. "Hey, didn't we leave it out this week?"

"Yeah." Peter tried to take the other end of the string. "I think Uncle Morten and Grandfather took it down when they started painting."

"Here." Henrik pulled at the string, "We should set it up again."

"That's just what I was thinking," agreed Peter. After a few minutes of untangling, they set it up just as Peter had the first time, leaving a string tightly stretched across where anyone walking close to the boat would trip over it.

"Perfect," Henrik pronounced, running his finger across the string. "Anyone who comes near here is going to pull those cans down."

The boys turned to each other and grinned.

"All set," Peter decided. "Let's go eat. Mom's going to have a good dinner ready."

14

VOICES IN THE NIGHT

Peter hadn't seen Elise smile so much in a long time.

"A toast to the prettiest flower girl in Denmark," said Peter's father, raising up in his chair. The bride, groom, pastor, and everyone else had already received their own apple juice toasts.

As everyone raised a glass, Elise turned bright red.

"I thought I was the only one in this family who could blush like that," whispered Peter. But the pastor's wife, a silver-haired woman in her midfifties seated across the table, overheard and laughed.

"Peter," commented Mrs. Andersen, who was sitting next to the pastor's wife. "You know blushing runs in our family."

"To the blushing Andersens," offered Henrik.

"Skoal!" Everyone agreed and clinked their glasses once again. "To the blushing Andersens. Cheers!"

"And one more toast," added Mr. Andersen while he was still on his feet. Peter thought he looked even happier than Elise. "To the cooks. This has been a supper to remember."

This time it was Mrs. Andersen's turn to blush. She had helped the pastor's wife by bringing over platters of Danish meatballs and gravy, potatoes, and shredded red cabbage.

The two women had cooked it together in the parsonage kitchen, then served it to the wedding party that evening. The group was crowded into a dining room barely large enough to hold a small dining room table.

"But this is just the beginning," announced Lisbeth's father, who had arrived in Helsingor earlier that afternoon. "The big dinner comes tomorrow, I'm told."

"That's right," added Mr. Andersen. "The big dinner comes tomorrow after the wedding, which—don't forget—starts at five at the cathedral."

"Skoal to the future, Mr. and Mrs. Andersen," offered Grandfather Andersen. Everyone joined in a sort of cheer as they clinked their glasses once again.

But Peter couldn't help fidgeting in the warm parsonage where Pastor Dalberg and his wife lived. While everyone else continued to give speeches, he wondered what might be happening down in the boatyard.

What if someone's out there right now? he thought. *Maybe Keld Poulsen is setting fire to the boat with his cigar while everyone's saying hurrah.*

It was almost nine o'clock, the time Henrik had heard Keld and Mr. Poulsen mention. And if Peter's uncle cared, he didn't show it. *All he does is look at Lisbeth with that silly grin.*

Henrik nudged him from the side. "Are you thinking what I'm thinking?" Henrik whispered into Peter's ear.

"Maybe," Peter whispered back. "Almost nine. I was thinking we should take a walk."

Henrik gave a thumbs-up sign. "Exactly. I'll slip out first. Meet you outside the door of the apartment in five minutes."

"Right," Peter agreed. "We'll be home before anyone else."

Henrik excused himself quietly as planned. While everyone was still chatting at the table, Peter got up to follow.

"Peter, sit down," ordered Lisbeth from the front of the room. Peter looked up, surprised. But Lisbeth was smiling, so he relaxed. She tapped the edge of her glass with a spoon, and the room became silent.

"You all know that Morten wants to launch the boat tomorrow after the wedding and the dinner," she began. "The men have all been working hard to get it done, and I think they deserve some extra credit."

Everyone clapped and Grandfather Andersen and Uncle Morten beamed. Lisbeth was right. They had worked extra hard.

"Morten wants to have a rechristening," she continued. "And he suggested I break a bottle of orange soda over the bow. Of course, we're not going to change the name, in honor of Morten's mother, but I think Anna Marie's granddaughter should have the honor."

Everyone looked at Elise and clapped while her face turned the color of a summer sunset.

"How about her grandson?" Elise argued. "He's the one who saved the boat from being burned."

It was Peter's turn to be embarrassed.

"Elise is a girl," said Peter. "She should do it." He wanted to, of course, but didn't want to look too eager in front of so many people.

Uncle Morten stood at his seat and fished a coin out of his pocket. "Well, there's only one way to solve the problem. Elise, since we all agree you are the girl, you get to call it."

Elise looked nervously at Peter. He just grinned back.

"Go ahead, Elise," he urged her.

"Okay," agreed Elise as Uncle Morten flipped a small copper penny in the air. "Tails."

Uncle Morten snapped the coin out of the air and slapped it on his palm. Peter looked over at the coin, face up with a picture of King Christian the Tenth.

"There's the King," announced Lisbeth. "It's heads. Peter's the one."

Elise patted her brother on the back and smiled at him, while

Peter picked up a half-full bottle of soda on the table in front of him.

"Okay, I'll practice with this bottle."

"Wait a minute," said Peter's father. "We don't want anyone to get hurt on broken glass, do we? Maybe you should just pour the bottle out on the boat, without breaking—"

"But . . ." Peter wondered if just pouring a bottle of soda on the boat would be a real christening.

"You're right, brother," agreed Uncle Morten, looking over at Lisbeth. "We don't want a lot of broken glass to clean up."

Peter shrugged. "Whatever."

"And now that we have that all figured out," continued Uncle Morten, "isn't anyone interested in some dessert?"

"Oh, I get it," teased Mr. Andersen. "You're just being agreeable so we can get to the rhubarb pudding."

Peter retreated to his chair, then looked out the window. *Henrik's probably out there wondering what's going on*, he thought. While everyone was busy getting their dessert, he slipped out the back door.

"What took you so long?" whispered Henrik after Peter was safely outside.

Peter motioned Henrik to follow him down the dark street that led to the harbor. "We had to decide who was going to re-christen the *Anna Marie*. Elise or me."

"Rechristen? You're going to name it something else?"

"No, same name. They just thought that since they were getting married and the boat was practically new again, that they should celebrate in a special way, I guess. New start, new boat. That kind of thing."

"Oh. So who gets to throw the bottle?"

"I do."

"Lucky."

"Yeah, but this better be worth it," Peter whispered to Henrik out on the dark street. "We're missing out on rhubarb pudding."

Henrik licked his lips. Peter knew it was his favorite, too.

"Maybe they'll save us some. But we should hurry."

The boys started to run along the narrow cobblestone streets, taking the shortest route to the harbor. When they got to the place where the *Anna Marie* lay in her cradle, they stopped to take a careful look around.

"Looks like a big dinosaur," observed Peter, taking a step toward the big, dark monster.

"Shh." Peter pulled him back and whispered, "They might be around. And watch out for the alarm!"

"Oh yeah," replied Henrik. "I don't see anything."

" 'Course not. It's too—"

Both boys froze when they heard footsteps coming toward the boatyard from behind them.

"Quick!" He pulled Peter up a small stepladder on the opposite side of the boat. They flopped noiselessly onto the boat's deck and crawled over to the new steering house.

"What if they start the fire below?" worried Peter. "We'll fry."

"Shh," warned Henrik. "We can always scream."

The thought didn't comfort Peter.

As the footsteps came closer, Peter was almost afraid to breathe. He heard them stop directly underneath the boat, and then heard a shuffling sound, as if someone was looking around. On the edge of panic, Peter was ready to jump up and yell—but Henrik held him down. Finally they heard the footsteps once again. As they grew fainter, the boys carefully popped their heads up over the railing.

"See anyone?" whispered Henrik.

Peter strained his eyes in the dark. He noticed a lone figure pass under a streetlight halfway across the boatyard, then slip into the front door of a warehouse.

"Over there," Peter pointed.

Henrik moved for the ladder, and they both slipped down without a sound. A minute later they crept under the window of the warehouse. Henrik was the first to look in.

"See anything?" asked Peter. He could see shadows playing

on Henrik's face from the dim light inside. There were voices within, two men's voices, but they were muffled.

Henrik shook his head and ducked down. "I can't see anything. Boxes in the way."

Peter took a turn peeking inside. Henrik was right—all he could see at first were boxes piled into tall stacks. There was a light somewhere behind the boxes, then a shadow moved, and someone came into view for a moment.

Peter gulped. It was Verner Norsk!

"I saw—" Peter began, but something fell in the boatyard behind them—a can, some boards, Peter wasn't sure what. He whirled around nervously, and they both crawled quickly behind a pile of empty oil drums near the front of the warehouse.

"What was that?" whispered Peter.

Just then, a boy lugging a large square gas can appeared under the lamp by the door. Peter was afraid to look and kept his head low. The boy stopped in front of the door, set the gas can down, and rapped three times.

"Dad, are you in there?" came the nervous voice of Keld Poulsen.

A moment later the door swung open, spilling light out into the boatyard. Peter tucked his head down tighter but kept his eyes on what was happening.

"Is this all of it?" came a man's gruff reply. "Get in here before that old security guard sees you."

Peter remembered the voice clearly from his time in the German prison. There was no mistaking it. It was Keld's father, Mr. Poulsen.

"Yeah," replied Keld. "This stuff came from a milk truck." Then he started laughing. "And you should have seen me. I had the tube in the tank to siphon the gas, and the milkman came out of the building and just drove off. He's not going to get very far, though. I cleaned him out."

"All right," snorted the man. "That's enough jabbering. You know the schedule."

"Yeah, but is that enough gas for the boat?"

This time Mr. Poulsen laughed; it sounded more sinister than his son's laugh. "It's enough to do the job, Keld. Now go home to your mother before she comes looking for you." And then the door slammed.

"But, Dad," Keld whimpered.

The boy stood in front of the warehouse door for a long moment, then turned away. Peter pulled his head back behind the barrel and they listened as Keld walked slowly out to the street.

"Wow, did you see that?" Peter whispered a few minutes later as they tiptoed away from the warehouse and back toward the *Anna Marie*. "They're going to use that gas Keld stole to burn up the boat!"

Looking back over his shoulder, Peter wanted to get out of there as fast as he could. But they couldn't just leave the boat.

"Come on," whispered Henrik. "Let's go up here to think for a minute." He circled around to the opposite side of the fishing boat to where Uncle Morten's ladder was still leaning against its side.

As Peter climbed up the ladder, he had the sinking feeling they were climbing up onto a bonfire waiting to be lit.

"Are you sure it's a good idea to be up here?" Peter hesitated at the top. "What if Mr. Poulsen comes again?"

"Well, we can't see him from anywhere else. Can't see him from the boathouse. Now that we know what's going to happen, all we have to do is—"

"I know I've said this before, but this is nuts, Henrik. We just need to get out of here. Mr. Poulsen's going to come up to the boat, pour the gas underneath, and *poof!* Why don't we just go back to the parsonage and tell someone?"

"Okay, okay, just let me think for a minute. There's got to be a way out of this."

"The way out of this is down that ladder. We need to go tell my dad and my uncle what's going on. The party's probably over by now."

"Wait!" Henrik grabbed Peter's arm. "What if Mr. Poulsen sets the fire while we're gone?"

"I don't know, Henrik." Peter crouched down low in the new deckhouse, keeping his eye on the warehouse. They had waited not more than five minutes when the door slowly opened and two figures stepped out into the dim light.

Mr. Poulsen was holding the same five-gallon gas can that Keld had delivered. Behind him, Frits was carrying a duffel bag. As Frits locked the door, Peter heard what sounded like arguing.

"That's all I get?" whined Frits. "I'm taking a lot of chances helping you. And if my Uncle Knud found out—"

"Oh, don't worry about it," replied Mr. Poulsen, walking down toward the *Anna Marie*. "You've done your part. You'll get your money. Now, how are we going to fire it up without making a lot of noise?"

"That's it. I'm not waiting to find out," Peter decided. He jumped out of their hiding place, slid down the ladder, and crumpled when he hit the ground. Henrik was right behind him, falling in a heap on top of Peter.

"Come on!" Peter hissed as he untangled himself. He got up and sprinted out of the boatyard. Henrik was right beside him, matching Peter stride for stride.

"Uncle Morten's probably home by now!" Peter managed to say once they were safely away from the boatyard. "His apartment." He was afraid to look behind him, but he glanced back every few yards to make sure the man with the gas can wasn't running after them.

His uncle's apartment was closest, only a block from the waterfront. But would he be home yet? They bounded up the stairs, pulling themselves up by the railings and taking two at a time.

"Uncle Morten!" Peter yelled, pounding on the door to apartment 201, the first door at the top of the stairs. "Uncle Morten! Open up!"

They waited a moment, breathing hard. An older woman

from across the hall yanked open her door.

"What's all the racket out here?" she demanded, drying her hands on a dish towel and looking cross. "Your uncle isn't home yet."

Peter looked over at the gray-haired woman, now standing with hands on her hips in the doorway and frowning. He tried to smile, but there wasn't time.

"Thanks," Peter managed.

"Sorry," added Henrik.

They flew back down to the street, barely touching a stair.

"Okay, he's probably still at the parsonage with everybody else," croaked Peter. But Henrik was already striding down St. Anne's Street toward the cathedral and the pastor's apartment next door.

"What if he and Lisbeth are out somewhere?" asked Henrik. Peter didn't have the breath to answer. He kept his head down and sprinted as if his life depended on it. He was afraid to look back again, or in the direction of the boatyard. He didn't want to see the flames.

"Do you think they saw us?" Henrik asked.

Again, Peter didn't answer. *There's no way Mr. Poulsen could have missed us crashing down out of the boat,* he thought.

Two blocks down St. Anne's Street, the boys reached the small apartment building next to the church. Cheery lights were streaming down to the street from the second-floor apartment, and Peter thought he saw the outline of his dad.

"Hey, watch out!" cried Mr. Andersen as they nearly bowled him over in the hallway by the door of the pastor's apartment. "I was wondering where you two had disappeared to. You even missed dessert."

Everyone was just coming out. Peter held on to his father's shoulder while he caught his breath enough to talk.

"Dad," Peter caught a breath. "I'm sorry." He took another big breath. "But we saw—"

"Keld's dad has a gas can." Henrik took up the story. "And he's going to set—"

"He's going to set the boat on fire," finished Peter. "We saw him. You've got to come help!"

Elise was laughing with her mother, Pastor Dalberg's wife, and Lisbeth in the apartment, but she stopped midsentence and stared out into the hallway.

"Where have you two been?" she asked.

"No time to explain." By this time Peter was catching his breath. "Uncle Morten, you have to hurry to your boat before they burn it up!"

"It might already be too late," concluded Henrik.

Uncle Morten glanced at his brother, then looked at the boys.

"I hope this isn't some kind of prank," warned Uncle Morten.

"No joke, Uncle Morten." Peter tugged his father's arm as they headed down the stairs. "We saw Mr. Poulsen. He had a gas can, and we heard them talking."

"Mr. Poulsen?" asked Uncle Morten. "You saw Erling Poulsen again?"

"That's what we've been trying to tell you." Peter led the way down the stairs and onto the street. "He and Keld are planning to burn the boat to get back at you."

Peter heard someone run up behind them as they jogged back down St. Anne's Street toward the boatyard.

"Elise!" Peter huffed. "You should have seen it. I thought Keld's dad was going to torch the boat while Henrik and I were hiding on it."

"Did he see you?" asked Elise.

Peter nodded. "Yeah, I think so. Look for smoke up ahead."

But there was no smoke to smell, no flames to see. And the boatyard was deathly quiet when the five of them arrived at the worksite. The *Anna Marie* still stood over the boatyard like a dinosaur on display—dark, tall, and quiet.

"So where's Mr. Poulsen?" asked Elise.

"Over there." Peter pointed toward the warehouse. "He came

out of there. Maybe he's still inside."

Uncle Morten took a quick look around, then headed off in the direction of the harbor office at the edge of the boatyard by the street. "I'm going to go find Madsen, the harbor master. Be right back."

He was back in a minute, followed by a grumpy Mr. Madsen.

"So, Morten says you kids thought you saw someone around here with a can of gas." The man snorted in his usual way when he spoke. "Not likely. But I hear there are a few kids who steal it right out of cars. It's still not easy to come by."

"But we know who we saw!" insisted Henrik. "Mr. Poulsen and his son Keld. We heard them talking about doing the job right, or something like that."

"You actually heard them say they were going to burn your uncle's boat?" The man leaned close to Peter's face. Peter winced and pulled back from the stern glare in the man's eyes.

"Well," Peter admitted. "Not exactly, but—"

"How about the gas," interrupted Mr. Madsen. "Did you see them pouring it onto your uncle's boat, or maybe someone lighting a match?"

"No, but we saw him by the boat," insisted Henrik.

"Yeah," agreed Peter. "We were up on top of the boat, and he was coming toward us with the gas can in his hand."

"How do you know it was this Poulsen fellow?" inquired Mr. Madsen. "Did you get a good look at him?"

"Well, kind of," answered Peter. "I've seen him before, and I thought it looked like him."

"So let me get this straight," concluded Mr. Madsen. "You didn't actually hear this man and a kid say they were going to set fire to your boat, but you're positive they are going to do it. You haven't seen this man up close. He was fifty feet away and in the dark, but you're positive it's him."

Mr. Madsen ran his hand through his hair and turned to Uncle Morten. "The only thing we can say for sure is that we have a couple kids here with very active imaginations."

"But what about the fire?" Elise stepped up from the shadows. "Somebody set that."

Mr. Madsen just shrugged. "I still think it could have been bad wiring. Maybe kids."

Uncle Morten cleared his throat. "Well, listen, Madsen, my nephew and his friend may not have seen an arsonist, but I think we should at least check out their story."

"Over there," Henrik pointed. "When we were here just a few minutes ago, they were doing something in that warehouse."

"That place?" Mr. Madsen shook his head. "It's always locked. Padlock. Here, I'll even show you."

They all walked over to the warehouse, and Mr. Madsen triumphantly pulled on a locked padlock.

"See? No one can get in here."

"But Mr. Poulsen was," Henrik insisted. "Can't you look inside?"

"All right, all right." Mr. Madsen grunted and fished around on his large, round keychain. He tried three or four keys before happening on the right one. "We haven't used this warehouse for much lately," he mumbled, finally throwing open the door with a squeak.

He snapped a switch and a bare light bulb cast a dingy circle of light on a pile of boxes. They looked just the way they had earlier, only no one was inside.

"Satisfied?" Mr. Madsen snapped off the light.

"Okay, they're not here now," said Mr. Andersen.

"If they ever were," finished the crabby security guard.

"If the boys say there were people here with cans of gas," concluded Uncle Morten, "then there were people here with cans of gas. I'd feel much better if you would keep an extra watch on the boat tonight."

Mr. Madsen put up his hand in a kind of salute. "I have no problem with that, Morten. You know I'm always looking out for trouble. That's my job. It's just that I can't be chasing ghosts all night."

Peter frowned and tightened his fists in the darkness. Mr. Madsen didn't believe them. Then something crashed behind them.

"Peter," cried Elise. "It's your alarm."

"The alarm!" echoed Peter, and he spun around to face the *Anna Marie*.

Mr. Madsen beamed his strong flashlight toward the boat, while Henrik and Elise circled around. There was a clatter of falling boards, then the sound of someone running off.

"It's not the alarm," shouted Peter. He ran toward the street, past the boat, and looked up all the streets. There were lights on in the waterfront restaurants, but only a few people were out on the streets. And no one was running away from the harbor.

"What was it?" asked Henrik, running up next to him. "See anybody?"

Peter shook his head as they returned with Elise to the boat-yard.

"Here," Peter pointed at a pile of boards that had been perched on top of a full trash bin. "Somebody was standing here and bumped against this pile of boards. Whoever it was must have been trying to get away in the dark."

"He's already gone," said Henrik, disappointed. "See, Mr. Madsen? There really is someone hanging around here. There's a boy about our age—except he's much bigger than we are. And there's Mr. Poulsen, his dad."

Peter could see the man's rough face soften for a moment. "Maybe you kids are right," he finally said in his gravelly voice. "We don't want anything happening here in the boatyard to-night."

"You'll keep an extra eye on the boat?" Uncle Morten asked the security guard.

"I said I would."

Satisfied, Uncle Morten turned away from the boatyard, fol-lowed by the others.

"Come on home, kids," called Mr. Andersen. "I don't think

we need to worry anymore. Mr. Madsen will keep an eye on things. We have a wedding to think about. And, Morten, you need to get a good night's sleep. Tomorrow's your big day."

Before he left, Peter took one last glance back to make sure the can alarm was still set.

15

FAR FROM THE STORM

"Henrik," Peter whispered in the darkness. "Are you still awake?"

There was no answer, so Peter sighed and rolled over. He hadn't been able to sleep since they went to bed. Maybe it had been all that running, but his heart was still racing. And every time his heart slowed down, his mind took over.

Peter could still see the outline of Mr. Poulsen coming at them with the can of gas. Once he almost fell asleep, but it was no use. He reached over, flipped on the lamp by his nightstand, and looked at his alarm clock. Midnight.

"Henrik?" Peter whispered once more. But a quiet snore told him Henrik was sleeping soundly. Tiger was curled up beside him.

Peter fumbled around in the nightstand drawer for his Bible. Propped on his elbow, he flipped open the well-worn book to the Psalms, his favorite.

I need a good one tonight, God, he prayed quietly. Closing his eyes, he flipped the pages and stabbed his finger down on the page. Elise had told him that God didn't speak that way, but he was too tired to care. When he looked back down at the page, he made out a verse from Psalm 55.

"I am distraught at the voice of the enemy," he read under his breath. "My heart is in anguish within me." He thought about Mr. Poulsen again, about Keld, and about the soldiers racing through the streets at the end of the war.

Lord, every time I think about those people, my knees start to shake.

In his mind he saw Tiger once more, lying in the street. Only this time he tried not to let the anger sweep over him the way it always seemed to when he started thinking about the people who had hurt him and his family.

I just want to forget about them, Lord, but I can't. Not by myself.

He skipped a couple of verses and kept reading.

"Oh, that I had the wings of a dove . . ."

That's what I want, too. Or maybe the wings of a pigeon would work okay. That way if I ever see another German soldier, or Mr. Poulsen, or Keld, I can just . . .

"I would fly away and be at rest. I would flee far away and stay in the desert."

That sounds just about right, God. I'd settle for a little island, maybe.

"I would hurry to my place of shelter, far from the tempest and storm."

I don't know where that place is, God. Can you show me?

Peter's eyelids started to feel heavy, and he decided to rest his forehead on his Bible for a moment before he read more. Even though he was tired, he felt better than he had for weeks. And even though a storm of trouble always seemed to find him, he knew God was with him.

Now, if only I had a dove's wings, he prayed once more. *Then I could fly away.*

The next thing he knew, someone was jostling him awake.

"Hey, Bible scholar, wake up." Henrik leaned over and shook Peter's bed.

"Huh?" Peter looked over at his roommate with a dull expression. He was lying on his Bible, and his face had wrinkled several pages. "What time is it?"

Henrik glanced over at Peter's alarm clock on the table. "Seven."

"Seven?" Peter checked for himself. "Seems as though I just fell asleep."

Henrik gave Peter a curious look. "Do you really read that? I haven't seen you—"

Peter straightened out the pages and kept looking down. He could still remember the verses he had fallen asleep on, the ones about flying away, far from the storm.

"Once in a while." Then he looked up. "No, actually I read it a lot. I like it. I like the Old Testament. The stories—"

"You understand them?"

Peter shrugged. "Not always. But they're good. Sometimes the people act strangely, but the stories are good."

Henrik reached over and picked up the book. "My dad calls it the *Tanach*. That's Hebrew for Old Testament. He used to give me lessons sometimes, teach me the names of the Jewish kings and all that. Before he got sick, I mean."

"Do you miss your dad?" asked Peter.

Henrik was quiet for a moment.

That was a dumb thing to ask. Peter bit his tongue. *I should have kept my mouth shut.*

But at last Henrik tried to answer, looking up from his pillow with serious eyes. "Yeah, I wish he were home. Mom and Dad both."

Peter nodded. "Sometimes I . . . I . . ." he stumbled for the right words, wishing he hadn't started to say anything. He wanted to tell Henrik he had prayed for his dad, but he felt awkward talking about that kind of thing with his friend.

"What?" Henrik sounded curious.

"Nothing."

"No, really. What were you going to say? Sometimes you what?"

Peter looked down at his Bible and opened it to the first page. He had written there in small letters the date he had prayed to follow Jesus, last summer at his cousin's farm. Deep down, he wanted to tell Henrik more. But his tongue felt tied in knots.

They both looked up as someone rapped on the bedroom door.

"Are you guys coming with me?" asked Elise. "I'm going down to the dock to check on the boat."

"Yeah!" agreed Peter, pulling off his covers and launching out of bed feet first. Tiger had found his way out of the room sometime earlier. "Wait just a minute."

"I'm not waiting," she called back. "You guys are too slow."

Both boys were out of the bedroom seconds later, stuffing pajamas into their pants. For a moment Peter looked back at his Bible.

I blew it again, he thought. *Why can't I be honest with Henrik about who I really am?*

At the window, Henrik was looking out toward the harbor.

"Think the boat is okay?" he wondered aloud before running out the door.

"I don't see any smoke," observed Peter, stopping himself to look out the window. "Maybe we survived one more night."

But Elise didn't hear them; she was already out the door and into the cool, salty, early morning air. Peter didn't even have his shoes on yet, so he sprinted after her and Henrik.

"Whoa," he called after them, picking up his feet. "It's cold out here."

"Think Mr. Madsen caught anybody last night?" Henrik asked Elise as they trotted down to the harbor.

"I don't think so," she answered. "We would have heard about it."

She fished a wadded cloth napkin from her pocket and unwrapped three slices of cheese. "Anyone want some cheese?"

"Sure," answered the boys.

As they turned the corner to the harbor, Elise was the first one to see the *Anna Marie*. "It's still there," she called back, trotting a little faster.

They stopped next to the boat, and Henrik walked all the way around.

"Hey!" shouted Henrik. "Someone set off the alarm last night. Look over here."

The other two ran around to Henrik's side of the boat and stared at the pile of strings and cans littered across the ground. "Here's where the cans came down," said Henrik, pointing at the pile.

"Looks as if we scared whoever set it off," observed Elise, walking along a string of cans.

"Yeah," grinned Peter. "He must have started running. It worked!"

Elise stooped to pick up one of the cans. "Kind of. But it didn't stop the person."

"It wasn't supposed to trap anyone." Peter tried to defend his invention. "It was just supposed to make a lot of noise. And if someone came to burn the boat down, maybe he was scared away. The alarm worked."

"Okay," said Elise. "But we should go see if Mr. Madsen heard anything."

"Think he's there?" Henrik wondered aloud. They trooped over to Mr. Madsen's warehouse office and waited as Henrik knocked.

"Mr. Madsen?" called Henrik. He rapped several more times, then raised his voice. "Mr. Madsen? Are you in there?"

"Try the door, Henrik," suggested Elise.

Peter reached in next to Henrik to try the doorknob, and it turned.

"Open," whispered Peter.

"Mr. Madsen?" The door squeaked loudly as Henrik nudged it open. Inside, Mr. Madsen was snoring comfortably in an old wooden office chair, his chin pointed at the ceiling, his feet on a battered desk, and his arms folded on his chest.

"What? Hey?" Mr. Madsen snorted and nearly fell out of his chair. "Who's there?"

"Just us, Mr. Madsen," explained Peter.

Mr. Madsen scrambled to his feet and straightened out his shirt.

"Right," he mumbled. "Must have dozed off a minute there."

"We were just checking on the boat this morning, Mr. Madsen," said Peter, leaning in through the door. "We—"

Elise put her hand on Peter's shoulder as if to say something. Peter looked back at her.

"We were just wondering," Elise put in. "You didn't hear anything last night, did you? Maybe near the *Anna Marie*?"

Mr. Madsen rubbed his unshaven chin and peeked out his dirty window. "Last night? No, not a thing. Your uncle asked me to keep an eye out, so I did. And the boat's fine. Don't worry about a thing. I was up all night. It's been quiet as a church."

"Okay, thanks, Mr. Madsen," replied Elise. "Thanks a lot."

She pulled the boys out of Mr. Madsen's dingy office, and they ran back up St. Anne's Street toward home. By that time, Peter's feet were freezing, even though the early morning sun was already starting to warm the day.

"So who set off the alarm?" wondered Henrik.

"I don't know," answered Peter. "But I think Mr. Madsen got a good night's sleep."

————

The rest of the day was a blur. To the florist for flowers. To the bakery for more rolls. To the butcher for a roast. To the bakery again for a cake, then back to the florist and over to the cleaners. Peter's mother sent the twins and Henrik on errand after errand, in between helping to cut and tie bows, cleaning the house, and running messages around town.

"After this, can I go down to the boat to help Grandfather?" Peter asked just before lunch. "Please? He probably needs lots of help."

Mrs. Andersen looked at her watch. "No, not yet. I still have plenty of other things for you and your sister to do. You seem to forget we're having a wedding this afternoon."

Peter groaned. Henrik was being a good sport, hanging around and doing everything the twins had to do.

"What are you worried about?" Elise asked the boys. "You don't have to be in the wedding on top of all this other work."

"Good thing," answered Peter, and Henrik nodded in agreement. It was fine for Elise to be the flower girl, but Peter wasn't sure he could handle walking into a church with all those people staring at him. He was sure Henrik wouldn't be too fond of the idea, either.

Mrs. Andersen got off the phone a minute later, and looked around for Peter.

"Peter and Henrik," she smiled. "One more thing."

Henrik did a low bow. "At your service, Mrs. Andersen."

"Good. I need you to fetch something at Mrs. Bustrup's place over on Esrum Street. Do you know where that is?"

"Sure, Mom," Peter answered. "Esrum Street's easy to find. What are we getting?"

"My punch bowl. She borrowed it for a brunch and never returned it."

"No problem, Mrs. Andersen," Henrik reassured her. "We'll get it for you."

"Now, it's a lot of heavy glassware, so be care—"

But the boys were already out the door and down the stairs. Esrum Street was on the other side of the city cemetery, away from the harbor a short ways.

"Bikes?" wondered Peter.

"Nope," replied Henrik. "We have to carry glass."

"Yeah, okay. Let's get the bowl in a hurry so we can go see what's going on at the harbor with Grandfather and the boat." Peter walked as fast as he could down the sidewalk, away from the water.

Henrik nodded. "They're probably getting the last stuff ready so it can go back into the water."

Ten minutes later, Henrik rang the doorbell of the fashionable newer apartment at 85 Esrum Street, and they waited as a little dog started yapping.

"Bruno!" came a woman's voice from inside. "Bruno, be quiet!"

The boys looked at each other in horror, and Peter knew in a moment that it was the same Bruno who had snapped at them weeks ago when they had been in line to buy bananas.

"Did she say *Bruno*?" asked Henrik over the sound of the barking dog.

Peter nodded solemnly.

But Bruno only barked more loudly as the woman opened the door carefully. Peter and Henrik were ready for the little brown dachshund, but they still backed up to the edge of the front step.

"Uh, hello," began Peter, over the noise of the dog. "Mrs. Bustrup? We're—"

"BRUNO!" yelled the same tall, regal-looking woman they had seen at the grocer's. As she held back her snarling dog, she looked at them and smiled. "I'm sorry, boys. I don't know what's gotten into Bruno. But you must be here for the punch bowl. Your mother called. Come on in, and I'll get it for you."

She left the door open, but Peter and Henrik stood frozen on the front porch.

"Oh, don't worry about him," she crooned, then bent down to put her face in Bruno's. "He's just a sweetheart, aren't you, Bruno? You'd never dream of hurting anyone, would you?"

Bruno looked around her head and showed his sharp little teeth at Peter. But Mrs. Bustrup didn't notice as she stood up and walked back into her apartment. When Peter and Henrik still didn't move from their spot on the porch, she turned to wave them inside.

"Come on in, please. I'll be just a minute. You can keep Bruno company. He's really very gentle."

Where have we heard that before? Peter wondered to himself. He looked at Henrik and they split up, tiptoeing in on either side of Bruno.

"Nice doggie," Henrik cooed at the dog, who tried to keep his eye on both boys at once.

Peter watched the dog suspiciously as he slipped in. "Nice Bruno. We're your friends, remember? Want a banana, boy?"

The boys stood stiffly by the front door for a few minutes as Bruno sized them up, his nose working overtime.

"I think he smells the cat, Peter," guessed Henrik. Bruno wrinkled his nose like a hunting dog.

"I'll be just a minute, boys," called Mrs. Bustrup from somewhere inside the apartment. "I know it's here in the pantry somewhere."

"Take your time," Henrik called back through his teeth.

But they didn't have long to worry. Bruno stood guard over the boys for only another minute before Mrs. Andersen's friend returned.

"Here you go," she said, presenting Peter and Henrik each with a large cake-sized box. She looked down at her dog with a mushy smile. "Oh, Bruno, you've made a couple of friends, haven't you?"

She noticed the dog sniffing Peter's leg with interest.

"You have a dog at home, do you?" asked Mrs. Bustrup. "Bruno can always tell."

"Cat," replied Peter.

"I see," replied Mrs. Bustrup, looking disgusted. "Well, the bowl is in one of those boxes, and the stand and cups are together in the other. Tell your mother thank you for letting me use it so long."

"Okay," Peter backed out carefully as Bruno made a rumbling sound in his chest. "Thanks, Mrs. Bustrup."

As they hurried down the front steps, Peter noticed Henrik was right beside him.

"Nice dog, huh?" Henrik hurried along.

"Real nice. He remembered us really well. I don't think she did, though."

They walked faster and faster, seeing who would be the first one back to the apartment. Walking turned to trotting, then to running, until each boy was all-out sprinting.

"Beat you to the lightpost," called Peter.

"We'll see," answered Henrik. Even though Henrik had always been the better athlete, Peter had grown over the past year. The two boys sprinted side by side down the sidewalk, then Henrik pulled ahead.

Three steps from the curb outside the Andersen apartment, Peter knew he had made a big mistake. Before he could stop himself, his toe caught on a cobblestone, and he was flying. He tried to hold up the box of glass, but it was too late.

"I beat—" Henrik turned back from the lamppost just in time to see Peter crash at his feet. The top of the box flew open and a pink glass bowl flew through the air before shattering into thousands of pieces on the sidewalk.

On skinned knees, Peter stared at the disaster.

"Uh-oh," whispered Henrik.

The door flew open and Mrs. Andersen stood still for a moment, silent. Her eyes filled with tears, and she turned away.

"Mom, I'm sorry," Peter called after her. "I didn't mean to. I-I'll pay for it out of my allowance."

Mrs. Andersen said nothing, just ran back up the stairs. Elise passed her mother as she ran down to see what had happened.

"Oh, wow, Peter," she whistled, looking at all the broken glass. "You really did it this time."

"At least the cups are still okay." Henrik lifted up his box hopefully.

"Did you know that bowl was a wedding present to Mom and Dad from Grandmother and Grandfather?" Elise asked her brother. "It was really fragile."

Peter went for a broom and a dustpan in the kitchen, but his mother was nowhere in sight.

"Yeah, well I sure found out how breakable it was," he told Henrik, who held the dustpan. "But I didn't know it was a present. I guess I should have."

Fifteen minutes later, after they had finished sweeping up all the glass from the sidewalk, Peter got up the courage to knock on the door to his parents' bedroom.

"You can come in, Peter," his mother said quietly.

Peter could tell right away she had been crying. Her eyes were red and puffy, but as she sat on her bed, she dried her face with a handkerchief of Mr. Andersen's.

"Mom, I'm really sorry," Peter began, standing awkwardly in the doorway. "I was being stupid. I-I didn't know it was a wedding present. I'm sorry."

Peter's mother closed her eyes for a moment, then looked into Peter's. "I'm sorry too," she began. "It was the only present I had left from your grandmother. It meant a lot to me." She blew her nose. "But I guess we can't hold on too tightly to things, can we? Especially glass things."

"I should have been more careful."

"Yes, you should have. But it's done now. I forgive you."

She must have seen the still terrified look on Peter's face, and she patted the bed next to her. "Come here. I said I forgive you."

Peter sat down next to his mother, and she put her arm around his shoulder. "But that doesn't mean you don't have to help me the rest of this afternoon. We still have a thousand things to do before the wedding tonight."

This time, Peter didn't groan.

16

WEDDING BELLS

" 'Meet you at four.' That was the last thing he told me," explained Peter. He paced nervously in front of the big tower of the Helsingor cathedral, where his uncle's wedding was due to start in a half hour. It was four-thirty.

Elise looked worried. "But he's going to be late if he doesn't make it soon. He doesn't want to miss the wedding, does he?"

"Of course not." Peter bobbed on his toes and wiggled in his Sunday clothes. It was too nice an evening to be wearing this kind of suit, he told himself. As soon as it was over, he would change his clothes as fast as he could. But Henrik was going to miss the wedding if he didn't hurry up.

"What time is it now?" Elise asked a few minutes later. Peter didn't answer, only looked up and down the street. People eyed them curiously as they pedaled by on their bicycles. Most smiled when they realized there was going to be a wedding. Then, in the direction of the harbor, Peter saw a rough-looking teenager slip toward the church.

"Elise," Peter whispered out of the corner of his mouth. "It's Frits again. He's walking toward us."

"Why are you whispering?" she asked as she slowly turned around to see who Peter was talking about.

"What's he doing up here, I wonder? I don't like it."

"I suppose he has just as much right to walk past this church as anyone else." Elise crossed her arms. "Just like your friend Henrik had better be doing if he doesn't want to miss the wedding."

Peter checked to see if Frits was getting closer, but the older boy was gone.

"Where'd he go?" asked Peter. "I'm sure he saw us. He was looking right at us."

Elise shrugged. Peter looked in through the church doors to where a clock hung in the lobby. More people were arriving all the time.

Suddenly, Elise clapped her hand to her mouth. "You don't think it's because Henrik doesn't want to come to a church, do you?"

"Don't be silly," Peter replied. He checked again for Frits, but gave up the search. "His family has been to Christian weddings before. He told me so. Just because they're Jewish—"

Peter's father stepped out to join them.

"Is the flower girl ready?" he asked. "She's needed in five minutes."

"Okay, Dad," Elise replied. She was wearing a flowery yellow dress with white lace trim and a matching white hat. Peter had to admit it looked pretty on her. Prettier than most dresses he had seen. Their mother had been up late at night sewing for the past week.

Elise turned to her brother before she went in. "You're supposed to sit up front with everyone, you know."

"I know, I know," Peter snapped back.

"You don't need to get mad."

"I'm not mad." Peter looked up and down the street. "Listen, you go ahead. I'm going to run back home and see if Henrik is okay. Maybe—well, I'll be right back."

Elise nodded and turned to go inside. "Hurry back."

It was only four blocks from the church to the Andersens'
apartment, but Peter couldn't move quickly in his stiff black Sunday shoes. Still, he covered the distance in less than five minutes
and pounded up the stairs.

"Hey, Henrik!" he shouted in the front door. "Aren't you coming?"

The apartment was silent.

"Henrik, are you in here?" Peter ran inside, checked the bath-
room and their bedroom, even looked in his parents' room.

No Henrik.

"Henrik, where are you?" He glanced at the kitchen clock and
nervously clapped his hands together once before running out
again. Tiger looked up from his basket, where he had been taking
a nap.

Fifteen minutes to five. Fifteen minutes before the wedding
would start.

"Tiger, you haven't seen Henrik, have you?"

Tiger meowed as Peter flew back out the door.

He looked left, then right, then started down toward the har-
bor. It was the only place he thought Henrik might have gone.
Could he be at Grandfather's boathouse checking on the pigeons?
No, he thought. *Better check the boat first.*

Down by the docks, everything seemed normal for a Saturday
evening. In the growing dusk, Peter saw a ferry returning from
Sweden in the distance, just beyond the long stone breakwater.
The cranes were silent—as they usually were for the weekend.
And someone was loading a small black powerboat at the end of
one of the piers near where the *Anna Marie* was pulled up.

In preparation for the celebration and launch later that evening, Grandfather had draped red and white streamers all over
the boat. But there was no sign of Henrik. Peter cupped his hands
to his mouth and yelled as loudly as he could.

"He-e-enrik!"

The two people down by the little boat whirled around, but

Peter couldn't see their faces. *Maybe they've seen where Henrik went*, thought Peter. He ran down closer to the docks.

But he didn't make it all the way. When he jumped onto the floating section of the dock, the boy who was loading bags of groceries into the boat stared straight at Peter. It was the last person Peter wanted to see: Keld Poulsen.

In an instant Peter knew who the man must be. Keld's father looked out of the back of the boat at Peter—and Peter froze in place for what seemed like a very long moment.

Wrong place, wrong time, Peter told himself as he spun around. He wondered if he would be able to outrun Keld. But as Peter sprinted back up to the boatyard, he heard the boat's engine roar to life.

He also heard someone pounding from inside a little tool shed perched in the shadows between a larger warehouse building and the *Anna Marie.*

"Hey, is anyone out there?" Peter heard Henrik's muffled voice as he ran by the shed.

For a minute he didn't know what to do. He had to tell somebody about Mr. Poulsen before he got away. But what about Henrik?

"Henrik?" Peter put his face up close to the solid wooden door of the shed. There were no windows anywhere, but there was a large knothole in the front at waist height where Peter could see Henrik's eye peering out at him.

"Peter? Boy, am I glad to see you. Mr. Poulsen locked me in here. Get me out, would you?"

Peter looked frantically down at the docks again, then tried the heavy padlock on the door. From inside, Henrik kicked and pounded on the door—but it wouldn't budge. The man from the boat was now running in their direction.

"I can't get it open!" Peter told him. "What do we do?"

"You get out of here!" insisted Henrik. "Run and get help. They're probably going to burn the boat down!"

"Hey, you!" cried Mr. Poulsen. "You! Peter! I just want to talk to you for a minute."

But Peter had heard enough. He turned and ran back toward the church as fast as his legs would pump. He had a good head start on Mr. Poulsen, but Peter knew the man would probably be able to catch up with him in a few steps if he wanted to.

Run! Peter told himself as he sprinted out of the boatyard and up St. Anne's. *Run!*

He had no idea what he was going to do if he made it to the church, only that he had to get help. He quickly glanced back over his shoulder to see how close Mr. Poulsen was getting, but he was nowhere in sight.

What? Peter wondered, slowing to a jog. *Why isn't he chasing me?*

"Watch it!" someone yelled in front of him just before Peter crashed into a bicyclist going the other way.

Peter caught the handlebars with his arm, swinging the bicycle and a teenage girl around and over on top of him. He ended up on the bottom of a pile of bicycle and one angry girl.

"Do you always run down the street looking behind you?" she scolded. She tried to get up, but her skirt was tangled in the bike chain.

Peter's best pants were ripped and his elbow was skinned, but he managed to crawl out from under the bike wreck.

"I'm really sorry," he explained, looking back once more in the direction of the harbor. "But th-there's an emergency, and I have to run."

"Hey," objected the girl, who looked fifteen or sixteen. "You can't just run off like that. Wait a minute."

"I'm sorry, really I am," Peter explained as he ran off. "But there's—"

Just then a low roar cut through the early evening air, and Peter froze in his steps. Even the girl on her bike stopped yelling to look in the direction of the harbor. An orange glow filled the sky, and it lit up billowing clouds of smoke.

Peter could only think of one thing. *Henrik. He's trapped, and they're burning who-knows-what. The boat? The shed?*

With a new strength he sprinted the last block to the church, slammed through the large wooden double doors, and ran into the sanctuary. His feet caught on the carpet runner and he almost lost his balance again.

At the front of the church, Lisbeth had reached the altar, where a pressed and handsome Uncle Morten was beaming at his bride-to-be.

Pastor Dalberg was the first to see Peter burst in looking like the survivor of a street fight. His calm expression turned to wide-eyed amazement as everyone in the church turned to see what was going on.

For a moment, Peter couldn't speak, he was so out of breath. Even the organist stopped in the middle of a note. The huge church was silent; only Peter's panting seemed to echo from the lofted ceilings.

"The . . . boat," Peter finally croaked, his hands on his knees. "Henrik's trapped!" Then he gathered one big breath. "I THINK THEY JUST BLEW UP THE BOAT!"

From his seat at the front of the church, Peter's father was the first to run out, followed by Elise and Uncle Morten. They gathered around Peter as he tried to run back to the door.

"What are you saying, Peter?" asked his father. "Where have you been?"

"What kind of a question is that?" asked Uncle Morten. "Look at the boy. Just tell us what happened, Peter."

"I can't," Peter said, trying to break free of his father's grip and the crowd that had now gathered around him. He was still breathing hard. "They locked up Henrik in a tool shed . . . couldn't get him out. Chased me. Big explosion. We've got to help!"

Uncle Morten and Peter's father looked at each other for a moment and nodded. By now the church aisle was full of buzzing people.

"Away from the aisle, everyone," yelled Uncle Morten. "Please stay here. We need out!"

Almost before Uncle Morten ordered them to move, people melted back into the pews, still buzzing with excitement. Peter led the way through the crowd and out of the church, flanked by his father and uncle. Elise was right behind them.

A handful of other men in ill-fitting tuxedos—fishermen friends of Uncle Morten—followed Lisbeth in her white gown. She pulled up the long train at the back of her fancy gown, kicked off her high-heeled shoes, and dashed after the odd parade of wedding-goers.

"Stay here, Lisbeth," ordered Uncle Morten.

"Not on your life, Morten Andersen." Her eyes flashed as she ran after him. Uncle Morten took one look at her and turned back toward the waterfront.

They had no trouble finding their way. A cloud of smoke and bright orange flames marked their destination. The area was filled with screaming fire trucks.

But all Peter could think of was Henrik, trapped in the tool shed. *Hold on, Henrik,* he pleaded. *Lord, please don't let him—* But he couldn't finish the prayer, afraid to think of what he was asking of God. He couldn't let himself imagine what he might see when they reached the boatyard.

When they got closer, they could see that the small warehouse building right next to the *Anna Marie* was in full flame, desperately near the boat. The tool shed where Henrik was still trapped was only an arm's length away from the flames, but it had not yet caught on fire.

"Where's Henrik?" shouted Uncle Morten. Peter pointed at the shed, ran around the flames, and pounded on the door.

"Henrik?"

"Hey, get me out of here!" Henrik's panicked voice rose above the roar of the flames.

Peter's father quickly surveyed the scene as if he was trying to judge what to do next. Peter looked for something they could use to pry open the door. The wailing sirens of more fire engines got closer.

"Where's Madsen?" shouted Uncle Morten. "He should be able to unlock the door."

But the security guard was nowhere to be found. Peter glanced quickly at the dock. The black powerboat was gone, and Keld had disappeared.

One of the walls of the larger building collapsed, sending a shower of sparks and burning wood in the direction of the shed where Henrik was trapped. Mr. Andersen put his arms around Peter as they crouched down.

"Dad, we've got to get him out of there!"

The heat from the flames almost drove them away as Henrik's pounding grew louder. A burning beam had fallen near the corner of the shed and was threatening to set Henrik's wooden prison on fire.

"I've got it," said Elise, staggering around from behind the shed. She was dragging an enormous beam of wood, as big as a small tree trunk and as long as a man. The front of her dress was wrinkled and dirty, but she didn't seem to notice.

"Elise!" cried her father. "How—?"

Elise didn't answer, just gritted her teeth and handed the end of the beam to her father. Uncle Morten groaned under the weight of the other end, but he managed to pick it up.

"Away from the door, Henrik," Peter shouted in through the knothole. "We're going to break it down."

"Right," answered Henrik. "Any time."

Uncle Morten and Mr. Andersen took a dozen steps back, then made a run at the door with their battering ram. Their beam smashed through the door at waist height, disappearing halfway inside. The wood splintered and creaked, but the door held.

"One more time," grunted Uncle Morten. Peter felt helpless as he looked from the tool shed to the burning building next to the boat. A breeze was starting to blow the flames toward the boat—the colorful streamers could burst into flame at any moment.

A few men from the wedding party had turned small hoses on the fire, but it was like spitting into the wind. For a moment, Peter wished they were back at the other dock by their grandfather's boathouse. At least there was a real fire hose there—the one they had used to put out the first boat fire.

"Hold on, Henrik," Lisbeth peeked in through the hole in the door. "We'll have you out in just a second."

She stood aside as Mr. Andersen and Uncle Morten finally smashed a large hole. A moment later they dragged Henrik to safety.

"There you go," grunted Uncle Morten.

Henrik looked around at the burning boatyard and wiped his forehead with his sleeve. Peter ran over to his friend and put his arm around Henrik's shoulders.

"Are you okay?" asked Peter.

"Wow," replied Henrik, sounding dazed. They both stared in wide-eyed fear as one side of the little shed where Henrik had been a prisoner caught fire. Then Henrik looked quickly around the boatyard.

"I know who set the fire!" he told everyone. "It's not who we thought."

But by then the flames were dangerously close to the boat, and no one seemed to hear Henrik's announcement.

"Elise," Peter pointed at the *Anna Marie*. "The boat's going to catch fire, too."

"Come on," she told him, pulling his sleeve.

A small shelter stood just above where the boat rested on her giant cradle with railway wheels. Elise and Peter ran over, shielding themselves from the intensity of the flames as they did. As the wind picked up, the flames burned ever closer.

"Which one of these lets the boat down?" cried Elise, pointing to a set of handles that controlled the machinery. From here, boatyard workers could raise or lower the cradle and the boats they wanted to pull out of the water.

Peter tried to keep down the panic that swelled up. "I think it's this one." Peter pointed to a large lever with a black handle. "No! That one! I've seen them work that before."

Elise grabbed the handle and tugged, but nothing budged. She put her hand up to her face as another flame licked closer. By that time fire trucks had pulled up at the other end of the boat-yard.

"Are you sure it's this lever?" she yelled, tugging once more. "We've got to let the boat down into the water, or it'll burn!"

Peter pulled at his hair. He felt sick and shaky from the panic. "Here, let me try."

He yanked on the lever just as Elise had done, but he couldn't make it budge, either. Sweat dripped down his forehead as he tried again.

"It's stuck," he coughed, looking up with frustration. The smoke made his eyes sting and well up with tears. He kicked as hard as he could at the rusty drum that held the cable from the boat cradle.

Everything around them was bathed in thick, foul-smelling smoke and the orange glow of the fire. To their left, between the burning warehouse and the water, Peter could tell that firemen were starting to conquer the flames.

As another part of the warehouse started to crumble, Peter saw someone dart out a small door facing the boat. In the awful smoke, Peter saw the frightened face of Mr. Madsen, followed by a second figure—Frits Norsk.

Even above all the noise, Peter heard Henrik's shout.

"That's them!" cried Henrik. "They're the ones who started the fire! I saw the whole thing!"

Mr. Madsen stiffened when he heard Henrik's shout. He turned to the left, but the harbor blocked his escape. Behind him, the building still burned wildly. And to his right Peter and Elise blocked the way.

Frits motioned to Mr. Madsen as they tried to slip around the back end of the boat to the street. But Mr. Andersen had caught sight of what was going on and ran around the boat to block the escape.

"Get back, kids," growled their father, suddenly face-to-face with Mr. Madsen and Frits. Up close now, Peter could see their clothes were blackened and their faces red and singed. Mr. Madsen's arms looked badly burned, as well.

"Look here, Andersen," Mr. Madsen puffed. A cigar hung crazily from the corner of his mouth. "What is this? I was running out to get some help." His eyes widened at the sight of Uncle Morten and Henrik, who had come up behind Peter's father.

"Henrik says he saw the whole thing," countered Mr. Andersen. "Why don't you tell us what you saw?"

"I did!" insisted Henrik. "I could see everything through the hole in the wall of the shed. They were carrying cans of gas up into the boat, and Mr. Madsen was laughing about giving Morten a wedding present he'd never forget!"

Mr. Madsen sneered at Henrik and nearly bit off his cigar. "You're going to believe this kid?"

"Then they went back into the building for more cans of gas," continued Henrik, mopping his brow. "Last thing I heard was Mr. Madsen yelling at Frits to put out his cigarette. And then, *boom!* I thought I was dead."

Mr. Andersen motioned to the twins and moved forward to take hold of Mr. Madsen. "Elise, Peter, move back out of the way. This man is going to explain the whole thing to the police."

Mr. Madsen smiled for a moment as he looked at the twins. "That's right, Elise. Just move."

But Elise was standing between two metal cables and couldn't move out of the way quickly enough as Mr. Madsen lunged for her. He grabbed her by the throat and held her out in front of him. Frits pushed Peter to the ground.

Elise gasped and kicked, but she couldn't make Mr. Madsen loosen his iron grip.

"Leave her alone!" ordered Peter's father, jumping forward.

"Move back!" answered Mr. Madsen, spinning around to use Elise as a kind of shield. "Let's just move back, so our little girl doesn't break her neck. I'll do it, you know."

Everyone froze as Elise gasped for air.

"Don't be foolish, Madsen," said Mr. Andersen, anger flashing in his eyes. "Let her go."

Mr. Madsen just motioned to Frits. "Make sure no one comes up behind us. You've already ruined things by blowing up our building instead of Andersen's wretched boat."

"What do you have against us, Madsen?" asked Uncle Morten, keeping his distance.

"Against you?" laughed the man. "It's payback time because of what you did to my brother Erik. I was going to give you and your new wife a fitting wedding present."

Uncle Morten looked puzzled. "Erik? I don't know any Erik Madsen."

"Oh yes, that's right," continued Mr. Madsen. "You Underground people would only know him by his code name, wouldn't you? Does the name 'Slim' mean anything?"

"Slim?" Uncle Morten finally replied, his eyes narrowing. "Slim was your brother? He was a traitor to Denmark."

Mr. Madsen snarled. "Maybe, but he was my little brother—and you . . . you killed him." Still trapped in the man's grip, Elise struggled to breathe in the smoky air.

"I didn't kill him, Madsen. He disappeared after he betrayed three good Resistance men to the Germans."

"You think I believe you?" Mr. Madsen looked like a wild dog trapped by hunters. "The last time I saw him alive he said he was going to meet you. Then he disappeared. That's how I know you're guilty. But I'm a reasonable man. I'm not going to kill you, just ruin you. Frits, get up there and finish the job, before those firemen notice what's going on here."

"But Uncle Knud," whimpered Frits. "What if it blows up too soon? You told me all I had to do was—"

"Quiet," snapped Mr. Madsen in the same blistering tone. "This boat would have been firewood by now if you hadn't fouled up twice! Two chances we had, and both times you ruined it!"

The crazed man continued to snarl and sputter, all the while tightly holding Elise. Peter tried desperately to think of something he could do, some way he could help his sister.

"Madsen!" called Uncle Morten. "This is just between you and me. Let her go!"

"No, I don't think so," retorted Mr. Madsen. "I want you and your loved ones to share this experience. Frits! Are you doing what I told you to?"

But Frits didn't have time to answer. Out of the corner of his eye Peter saw someone hurtle out of the smoke, knocking Mr. Madsen and Elise over like bowling pins. While Mr. Madsen struggled with a new attacker, Elise rolled to the side. In the confusion, Peter saw Keld Poulsen scramble to his feet.

Uncle Morten didn't hesitate; he flew at Frits and quickly wrestled the teenager to the ground as Mr. Madsen rose to face Keld. Peter's dad came from behind, but was too late to reach Madsen.

"Get out of my way," hissed Mr. Madsen. He shoved the boy aside and tried to escape around the water side of the boat—just as the gears Peter and Elise had tried to move made a loud popping and grinding sound. Finally free to roll, the *Anna Marie* jerked, shook, and coasted back to the water, down toward the bay. And as the boat picked up speed, the big-wheeled cradle holding it hit Mr. Madsen's leg from the side and sent him sprawling.

"It's going to roll over him!" shouted Henrik.

But Mr. Madsen quickly reached up and hung on to the boat cradle as it plowed toward the water, threatening to crush anything in its way. Instead of jumping clear, he was dragged down the ramp toward the harbor as the boat picked up speed.

Everyone watched helplessly as the fishing boat hit the water with a huge, dark splash, sending waves in every direction. The cradle and Mr. Madsen disappeared into the water. And as if nothing had happened, the *Anna Marie* bobbed free of the cradle and gently nudged the dock by the launching ramp. But Mr. Madsen didn't appear.

"Arne, pull the cradle back up!" yelled Uncle Morten from where he was pinning Frits to the ground. "Maybe he's trapped."

"What if we hurt him by pulling it up?" asked Elise, joining Peter and Henrik by the water.

Uncle Morten frowned and looked back again to where Peter's father had jumped to the controls of the boat cradle. He pulled Frits to his feet, locking the boy's arms behind him. Frits made no attempt to get free.

"She's right, Arne. We don't know where he is under there. Might be under one of the wheels."

As he watched the dark water bubble, Peter knew they didn't have much time. For a second, he thought he saw a fingertip reach up through the water, but he wasn't sure. Without looking around, he waded quickly into the cold harbor, pulling his way along the metal beam of the boat cradle.

"Peter!" cried his father. But Peter caught sight of the finger once again.

"Dad," he yelled back. "I see him."

Peter fixed his eyes on the spot just ahead of him where the hand had floated up. Someone splashed in behind him, but Peter refused to take his eyes off the spot. There was a drop-off, and Peter almost lost his footing in the soft mud. He took a deep breath and ducked under, feeling frantically for Mr. Madsen.

As Peter groped deeper and deeper, panic began to set in. *Where is he?* he asked himself. *And what do I do if I find him?*

The water was just deeper than Peter could reach, and his lungs started to burn for air.

Just a little farther. He's got to be here. Lord, help!

When he couldn't stand it for another second, his fingertips brushed against something soft, like a shirt. But Peter was already

on his way up. He grabbed what he could of the shirt and tried
to put his feet down, but hit mud.

For a moment Peter thought he might pass out. His lungs
were screaming. Instead, he kicked with the last of his strength
and pulled hard with his free hand.

A second later he popped out of the water, gasping for air. In
his left hand he yanked up the rag doll that was Mr. Madsen, and
with his right hand he paddled furiously to stay afloat. He
wished he had taken off his black shoes.

"Peter!" Mr. Andersen was treading water next to his son. He
grabbed him with two strong arms and guided him to shallower
water.

"I've got him, Dad." Together, they pushed Mr. Madsen toward shore.

Elise and Henrik both came splashing into the cold, dark water, grabbing Peter around the shoulders.

Elise held on tight as her brother stumbled in the shallows.
"Are you okay, Peter?" she asked him.

He nodded and gasped. "Just cold. The water's cold."

Their father dragged the unconscious Mr. Madsen up onto a
concrete work area, turned him on his stomach, and slapped him
on the back.

"Is he alive?" asked Henrik, crouching next to the body.

Mr. Andersen didn't answer, just kept on slapping the man's
shoulder blades. A moment later Mr. Madsen gagged, coughed,
and rolled over with a moan—as if he was waking up.

"Oh," he groaned, then coughed again. He tried to sit up, but
Peter's father held him down.

"Don't move," commanded Mr. Andersen. "You're okay."

"Oh-h, my head," sputtered the man. "Something hit me.
What's going on?"

"You nearly drowned, that's what," answered Mr. Andersen.
"And maybe we should have let you. But my son saved you."

Mr. Madsen tried once more to sit up, and this time he was
allowed to straighten out.

"Who pulled me out of there?" he mumbled slowly.

Peter pulled back from the small crowd that had gathered around Mr. Madsen, but the man caught his eye. In spite of his puzzled expression, there was a hard, cold look about him. Peter had to glance away.

"You jumped in after me?" asked Mr. Madsen, coughing and sputtering. He took a few more breaths. "Why did you do that?"

Peter just shrugged and shivered.

"I tried to stop him," Peter's father answered for him.

"I would have, too," put in Uncle Morten. He had found two pieces of rope and was tying Frits' hands behind his back. Behind them, the flames were hissing and snapping as firemen poured on more water. All that time, and no one had noticed the drama next to the *Anna Marie*. They had been out of sight behind the fishing boat.

Mr. Madsen took a deep breath and tried to stand, but tipped over backward. "Listen, Andersen. Maybe we can just forget this whole thing. I was leaving town, anyway. I can get you money if that's what you want—"

"Save it," Uncle Morten cut him off. "You're not going anywhere, except to the police."

With the two Andersen men standing over him, Mr. Madsen had little choice. He sighed and stayed where he was.

"They'll be interested in knowing the whole story," added Mr. Andersen. "Especially about how you and your nephew here took care of the harbor."

"It wasn't my fault," squeaked Frits. "I'm not going to take the blame. It was your idea to burn the boat in the first place, and—"

"You keep out of this," scolded Mr. Madsen. "What do you know about anything? You're just a little—ow!"

Uncle Morten finished tying a tight knot in the rope around Mr. Madsen's wrists and turned to the twins.

"Peter, Elise, are you okay? Henrik? How about you?"

All three nodded.

"Even your neck, Elise?"

Elise nodded once more, rubbing her neck. Her dress—ruined earlier—was now beyond hope. Her face was dirty, and her hair a mess. "It hurts, but I'm okay."

"Morten," called a voice from the street.

Lisbeth, thought Peter. *Where has she been during all this?*

"Morten, where are you? Are you all right?"

"Down here," replied Uncle Morten. A moment later Lisbeth—still in her now-rumpled wedding gown—ran up to Uncle Morten. Two dark-suited policemen were at her heels.

"Morten, are you all right?" Lisbeth was near tears, and Uncle Morten held her in his arms. "I . . . I saw what was happening, so I ran off to get the police. We came as quickly as I could get them to believe me."

"Everything's okay," he told her in a reassuring voice. "You did the right thing. We just had to launch the boat a little early, that's all."

Peter's dad stepped up to the police officers, who were looking in amazement at the group of people dressed in their Sunday finest, the fire, and the scowling Mr. Madsen with his unhappy nephew.

"You better explain this to me," said one of the men. Peter's father stepped up to the officers as Lisbeth began to cry.

"Oh, Morten," she began. "Our wedding is ruined."

Uncle Morten put his arm around his almost-wife. "Maybe we can invite everybody to come back again."

"But, Uncle Morten, that's not fair!" insisted Elise, putting her hands on her hips.

"Not fair?"

"No, it's not." Peter could see his sister's eyes flash with anger. "They almost took the *Anna Marie* away from you. You can't let them take your wedding away from you, too!"

Lisbeth took her hand. "Elise, honey, I don't know what other choice we have."

"And you've been through a lot," added Uncle Morten.

"Me?" Elise sounded amazed. "I'm fine. I'm just upset that someone can ruin your wedding just because . . . just because—"

"Come on, Elise," offered Peter. "Let's go see if the boat's okay."

"You go," fumed Elise. She crossed her arms and remained with Uncle Morten and Lisbeth while Peter and Henrik checked the boat. By that time, several of Uncle Morten's fishermen friends had gathered around to compare stories.

17

I Do

"Looks as though that's the end of the mystery," offered Henrik, climbing down into the boat behind Peter.

Peter looked back once more at the smoking building and wrinkled his face. "Not quite," he answered. "What happened to Keld and his dad? That was some tackle."

"Oh, yeah!" whistled Henrik. "His dad was the one who threw me in the shed when I saw them loading up their boat. I was just coming down to see if the *Anna Marie* was ready. I guess he didn't want me to tip off the police before he got away."

"Boy, you sure saw everything tonight, didn't you?"

"Yeah," answered Henrik. "Except what happened to Keld. I think we should ambush him and find out what he knows about all this."

"No." Peter shook his head and looked up at his friend. "You heard Mr. Madsen. They didn't have anything to do with the fire."

Peter was tired, but he knew something inside felt different. Somehow the anger had washed away when he jumped into the cold harbor. All the hate he'd been feeling for the people who had hurt them—the soldiers who had taken their country and almost killed Tiger, Mr. Madsen, and even Keld Poulsen—was gone.

"What do you mean, you don't think so?" Henrik sounded amazed. "We're not going to let Keld just walk away from this, are we? I was almost killed in that shed!"

Peter wasn't sure he could explain to Henrik how he was feeling.

"I thought you were the one who hated him so much," continued Henrik.

"I guess I used to."

"So I don't get it."

Peter sighed. "I'm not very good at explaining things."

Peter still didn't know how to tell Henrik. He wasn't sure if he understood it himself. All he knew was that he felt very different inside. They sat on the boat for a minute and looked back up at the boatyard. More and more people were gathering around Uncle Morten and Lisbeth.

"Can you see what's going on up there?" asked Henrik.

Peter squinted at the gathering crowd. It seemed as if there were thirty, maybe forty, people.

"I don't know," replied Peter. "Maybe they're coming to see if the fire is out."

"Someone needs to tell them they're a little late," said Henrik, hopping down from the boat. "They can all go home."

Pete heard laughter from the group, and the loudspeaker voice of Pastor Dalberg.

"We waited as long as we could, Morten," announced the pastor. "Some of us thought you got cold feet, but then somebody suggested that if you weren't going to come to the wedding, the wedding should come to you."

"After all, we have all this food," said Peter's mother, holding up a large serving plate covered with a towel. "I didn't work for days to have it go to waste!"

Everyone laughed, and then Elise came bounding down to the dock where Peter and Henrik were standing.

"Mom brought us some dry clothes," Elise told Peter, the excitement bubbling up in her voice. She had already changed out of her ruined clothes and into a school dress. "She said for you to change in the boathouse."

Peter and Henrik looked around at the wedding party with amazement. Mr. Andersen had joined the group and stood next to his brother.

"Well?" he asked Lisbeth. "I think my daughter is right. It's not fair to have your wedding taken away from you."

Uncle Morten looked around at the crowd and grinned.

"Well, I've never performed a wedding on a boat before," said Pastor Dalberg. He put his hands on Uncle Morten's and Lisbeth's shoulders. "But what do you say to finishing this up?"

The crowd cheered as if their favorite soccer team had just scored the winning goal.

"They're going to get married on the boat!" announced Elise.

"Okay," agreed Uncle Morten. "But let's just move the boat over to our dock, away from this mess."

While willing hands helped untie the *Anna Marie*, others walked around to the Andersen boathouse and pier, a few minutes away. To the cheer of the crowd, the boat's engine started and Uncle Morten motored swiftly away from the work site and back over to their home pier.

Dozens of people carried food in their arms. Others set up tables. Caught up in the excitement, Peter, Elise, and Henrik followed the party through the boatyard back to Grandfather Andersen's boathouse.

"Your father told me what happened over there," said Mrs. Andersen, rushing up to Peter with an armload of dry clothes.

Peter looked down. "It was nothing, Mom. Dad was right there."

"You scare me to death, the things you do," she told him.

"But he saved that guy's life, Mrs. Andersen," said Henrik.

"I know. I still can't understand why your father didn't stop you, though." Then she straightened up and handed Peter her bundle. "Here, I brought you some dry clothes from home. It looks as if your uncle is getting married, fire or no fire."

Already Pastor Dalberg had climbed onto the boat with Uncle Morten and Lisbeth. Elise stood proudly beside Lisbeth, holding a slightly wilted bouquet. Henrik was near the happy couple, too, listening.

Peter slipped into the boathouse to quickly change into the clothes his mother had brought him. The pigeons stirred as he buttoned his shirt, and then someone followed him inside. In the darkness the other person didn't notice Peter, but Peter could see Keld Poulsen's outline clearly as the other boy peeked out the window at the wedding.

Peter backed up quietly into the corner, wondering what to do. He could yell, but Keld would just run. As he stood thinking, the other boy's square shoulders shook, and for a minute Peter thought the boy was laughing.

In between sobs, Peter thought he heard Keld mumbling something to himself.

"Why did you have to leave?" said Keld, his shoulders still shaking. "Mom's never home. She doesn't care. You just messed things up. I should have come with you, but no, you wouldn't let me. . . ."

Keld kept crying and mumbling as Peter hid in the dark corner. Then one of the pigeons fluttered from its perch, and Keld whirled around.

"Who's there?" he growled and tried to wipe the tears from his cheeks with the sleeve of his shirt. But by then his eyes must have been used to the darkness, and Peter couldn't hide.

"What are you doing here?" asked Peter, stepping forward nervously.

"Oh, it's you." Keld turned back to the window as though nothing had happened. "Just watching. You have a problem with that?"

"No problem," Peter answered. He wondered why Keld didn't try to leave. Down on the dock the crowd started singing a Danish wedding song. "Know this song?" he asked.

"Are you kidding?" answered Keld, looking out the window. "I've never been to a wedding on a boat before. Never been to a wedding, period."

"Serious?" Peter smiled in spite of the situation. "Me neither."

They stood for a moment and listened to the singing. Peter could hear his uncle's deep voice, belting out the words slightly off-key.

"Um, I'm sorry about your dad." Peter searched for the right thing to say.

"No you're not. He just ran . . ." Keld's voice trailed off, and he looked back at Peter. "Look, I know what you're thinking, but I had nothing to do with the fire. Neither did my dad."

Peter nodded down at the group of people by the boat. "Okay, so why did you lock up Henrik? He nearly got killed."

"I'm sorry, all right?" Keld tried to slip past Peter to leave, but Peter stubbornly blocked the way. *I don't care if he knocks me down*, thought Peter, putting his hands on his hips. To his surprise, Keld stopped short.

"We had to. I just had to help my dad get out of here," Keld explained. "The police were after him."

"And what about Frits?"

"He was just helping my dad get a boat. My job was to get gas, and Dad paid him not to tell anybody. Not even his uncle, Mr. Madsen."

Peter shook his head. "And at the same time, Frits was helping Mr. Madsen with the fire business."

"I already told you," Keld defended himself. "I don't know what that fire was all about, and that's the truth. I'm sorry for the way things turned out. That's all. I've got to leave now."

"I'll bet the shoe wasn't yours, then, was it?" Peter ventured still another question. "And the handwriting on the notes wasn't yours, either. I'll bet Mr. Poulsen had Frits write it. He probably made it look like a kid's writing so we would think it was someone else."

Keld just gave him a blank stare as he shifted nervously from foot to foot. "What is this, Twenty Questions? I don't know what you mean by shoes and notes."

Peter shook his head. "Okay, forget it. The shoe must have been garbage, after all. Probably didn't mean anything. But you still haven't told me why you tackled Mr. Madsen when he was holding Elise."

The big boy just shrugged and sniffled. "I don't know. I just did." He dried the last tear from his eye with the corner of his sleeve. "But you keep asking me questions, and I have to go."

"Wait a minute, Keld," said Peter. He swallowed hard to get the lump out of his throat. "I've got to tell you one more thing. No more questions. Just—"

Peter remembered how Keld had always bullied him and Henrik. How Keld had helped the Nazis catch him and Elise when they were delivering Underground Resistance newspapers. Then he remembered his mother, forgiving him for breaking her glass punch bowl. This was no glass bowl, but . . .

"I have to tell you this. We thought you were the one who was trying to set my uncle's boat on fire. Now I know you weren't. I just wanted to tell you I'm sorry."

Slowly, mechanically, Peter took a step toward the other boy. It almost hurt. He knew what he had to do, but he couldn't make himself do it.

Lord, I can't forgive him, Peter cried silently. Something inside wouldn't let go. *But I can put out my hand. Please help me do the rest.*

It felt heavy and wooden, but Peter slowly stretched out his hand.

"Listen, it's okay—and I'm sorry, Keld." Peter forced the words out of his mouth, and then they tumbled out. "I'm sorry about your dad and about everything else, too. I'm sorry about everything."

Keld just stared at Peter for a long minute. He didn't take Peter's offered hand, but he didn't move, either. By then the singing had stopped, and Peter heard footsteps outside. The door flew open, and Henrik stood outside.

"Peter, where have you been?" called Henrik. "Everyone's looking for you. It's time to christen the *Anna*—"

Henrik caught sight of the other boy and stopped mid-sentence.

"What's *he* doing here?"

Keld straightened up. "Nothing. I was just leaving."

"No, wait a minute," Peter grabbed Keld's arm, and the forgiveness he had never known finally hit Peter like a warm flood. It hit him so hard, so unexpectedly, that it brought tears to his eyes.

"It's okay, Henrik," Peter told his friend. "Really, it's okay. Keld is going to help us with the christening. He already helped us with launching the boat, right, Keld?"

For the first time, Keld managed a stiff grin to match Peter's broad smile. "Yeah, I guess I did, didn't I?"

"That's right," Peter reassured him. By then the warm feeling had taken over, and there was no doubt what had happened. He stepped out toward the dock and the wedding party, Keld and Henrik in tow. He wasn't sure if Keld would come along, but he tried to sound sure of himself. "Come on, you guys. You have to help me with this."

Henrik's face showed his confusion, but he followed Keld and Peter back to where everyone had gathered around the front of the *Anna Marie*. Uncle Morten was making a speech.

"This isn't quite the way we planned it," he told the crowd. "We were going to launch the boat in the traditional way, from the shore. As you all know, it didn't happen that way. But thanks be to God, here we are. Only where is my nephew to rechristen our boat?"

Peter found his way through a knot of people next to the *Anna Marie*. Elise spotted Keld behind him, and her eyes nearly popped out. She turned and whispered to her mother.

"Oh, good, Peter," continued Uncle Morten. "There you are.

And there's . . ." His voice dropped off just as Henrik's had when he saw Keld.

"I'm ready, Uncle Morten," announced Peter, stepping up to the boat where his uncle was standing with Lisbeth and the pastor. "Only I think Keld should do the honors."

"Keld?" Uncle Morten held a bottle of orange soda uncertainly in his hand.

"Me?" echoed Keld.

"That's right," replied Peter. "He's the one who kept the boat from burning. Or at least, he's the one who saved Elise. Right, Elise?"

Elise nodded nervously, but Peter saw she was catching on. Uncle Morten handed the bottle over to Peter, and Peter passed it on to Keld.

"Me?" repeated Keld, looking at the bottle. "What do you want me to do? I thought this was a wedding."

Peter laughed. "It was. But now it's a family boat christening. Kind of a new start for everyone. Go ahead."

Keld looked nervously around at all the people, then shrugged. "All right, if that's what you want me to do. Just break the bottle across the front?"

Peter started to explain to Keld what his uncle had told him about rechristening the boat.

"No, all you have to do is pour a little orange pop down the front. We're not going to break—"

But Keld was already on the dock and had stepped up to the pointed front of the boat. He bent over like a batter looking for a home run.

"Wait," said Elise. "You're only supposed to—"

It was too late. Keld took a mighty swing and heaved the glass bottle straight at the bow with a grunt. His aim was right on target, and the glass shattered in a thousand slivers as orange soda splattered into the water. Everyone applauded.

"I think he's done this kind of thing with bottles before," Peter heard Henrik whisper. "In the street, you know?"

"Shh," scolded Elise.

"I christen you . . ." Keld began, then he looked around at everyone staring at him. "Hey, what's this boat called? Oh wait, I remember. I rechristen you . . . the *Anna Marie*."

EPILOGUE

Many of the events in this book actually happened. The war really did end for the little country of Denmark on May 4, 1945. The people really did dance and sing and wave their flags. The troops really did come home to Helsingor the way the book described, and there really were small battles in those first days after the war officially ended.

There were bitter feelings to get over, as well. Over five long years, the war had caused a lot of damage and changes in Denmark. People had been killed. The Germans were seen as villains, even hated. And the very few Danish people who had helped the Germans were immediately arrested. It wasn't easy to get back to normal after such a terrible time.

Most of all, the Danes learned that while wars can start very quickly, they take much longer to recover from. Sometimes years.

The hardest thing for people after the war was learning how to forgive. And as some discovered, the only way to truly forgive others is to first know God's forgiveness. Then we can find our place of shelter, "far from the tempest and storm."

The war's storm was over for Denmark. But for Peter, Elise, and Henrik, the adventures were only beginning!